W9-BXW-634

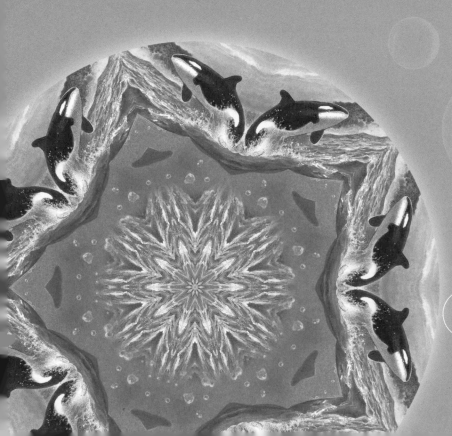

What parts of the front cover picture do you see in the design to the left?

Can you find the elements of earth, air, and water?

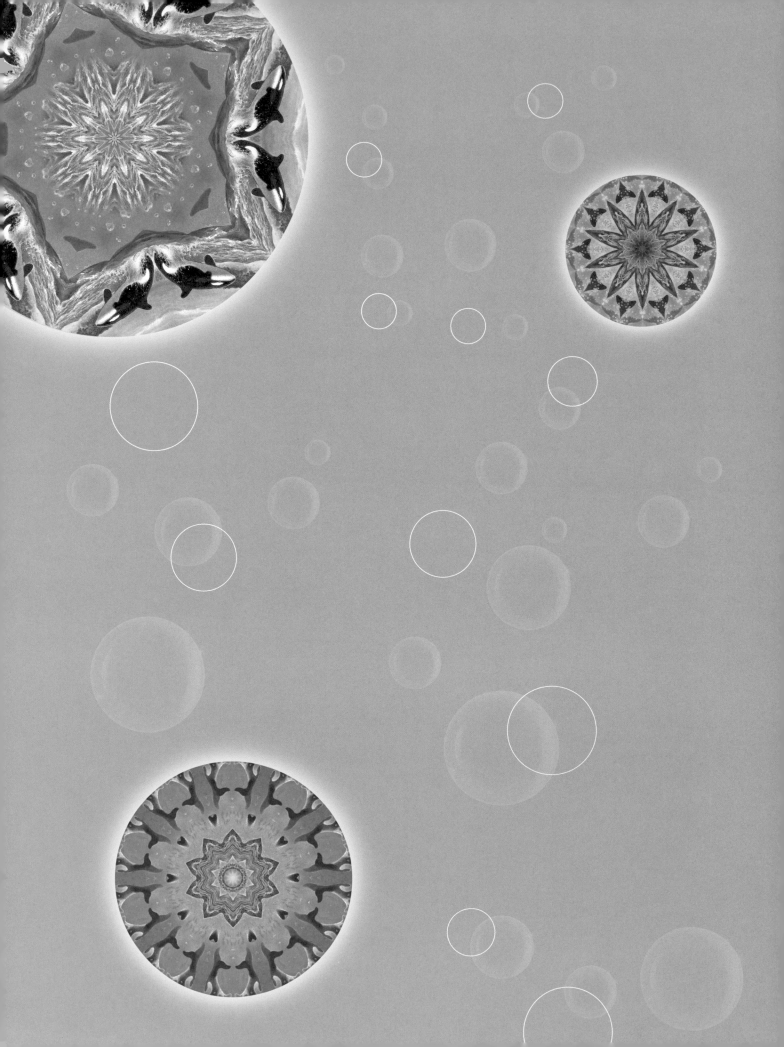

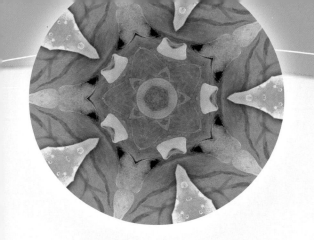

Literacy by Design™

Sourcebook
Volume 1

Program Authors
Linda Hoyt
Michael Opitz
Robert Marzano
Sharon Hill
Yvonne Freeman
David Freeman

Rigby®
A Harcourt Achieve Imprint

www.Rigby.com
1-800-531-5015

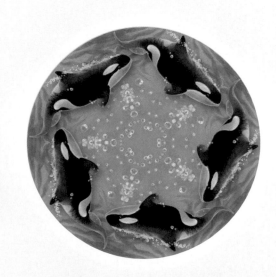

Welcome to Literacy by Design,
Where Reading Is...

Thinking

Discovering

Questioning

Literacy by Design: Sourcebook Volume 1
Grade 5

ISBN-13: 978-1-4189-4040-9
ISBN-10:   1-4189-4040-2

Printed in China
1 2 3 4 5 6 7 8   985 13 12 11 10 09 08 07 06

Imagining

Exploring

UNIT Road to Freedom

THEME ② Creating a New Nation Pages 34–63

v

UNIT Thinking Like a Scientist

THEME ③ How Does Cooking Work? Pages 66–95

Modeled Reading

Shared Reading

Interactive Reading

THEME ④ **What Is Sound?** Pages 96–125

Modeled Reading

Shared Reading

Interactive Reading

UNIT ▸ Proud to Be an AMERICAN

THEME ⑤ Let Freedom Ring
Pages 128–157

Modeled Reading

Shared Reading

Interactive Reading

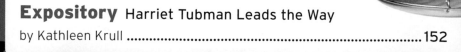

THEME 6 Balancing Act Pages 158–187

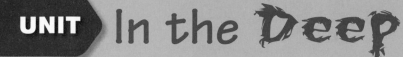
UNIT In the Deep

THEME ⑦ Ocean Life
Pages 190–219

THEME ⑧ **Bottom of the Deep Blue Sea** Pages 220–249

Washington Crossing the Delaware, 1851
Emanuel Gottlieb Leutze (1816–1868)

Road to Freedom

THEME **1** **A Call for Freedom**

THEME **2** **Creating a New Nation**

Viewing

The artist who painted this picture was Emanuel Gottlieb Leutze. He was born in Germany but grew up in the United States. He painted pictures about U.S. history. This painting shows General George Washington and his troops crossing the Delaware River in the winter of 1776. The event happened almost 50 years before the artist was born.

1. What challenges do Washington and his men face in the painting?

2. What feelings do you think the painter intended to create in the viewer?

3. Americans declared their independence from Britain in 1776. But it took years of fighting before they were actually free. Look at the soldiers in the painting. What clues help explain why the war took many years to win?

In This UNIT

In this unit, you will read stories about the American Revolution and the Declaration of Independence. You will look at events through the eyes of people from that time period. You will also read about how those events touch people's lives today.

CONGRESS, JULY 4, 1776.

Declaration of the thirteen united States of America

THEME 1

A Call for Freedom

Contents

Modeled Reading

Shared Reading

Interactive Reading

Dangerous Crossing:

The Revolutionary Voyage of John Quincy Adams

by Stephen Krensky   illustrated by Greg Harlin

JOHN AND ABIGAIL ADAMS

Please Don't Marry Him!

When Abigail Smith married John Adams in 1764, her mother was not pleased. Mrs. Smith believed that John was not the right match for her wealthy young daughter. Abigail knew better. Abigail and John settled down to a quiet life on a farm near Boston. However, growing **conflict** between the colonies and Great Britain soon **splintered** the couple's peaceful life.

Girl Power

John was one of the **representatives** to the First and Second Continental Congresses. John helped plan **military** action against Great Britain. During these long months, Abigail stayed home to run the farm.

Did you Know?

In 1765, Great Britain passed the Stamp Act. The act placed a tax on printed materials, including legal papers. The act hurt John's law practice. It also angered many colonists. John responded by helping to lead protests against the act. Over time, John came to believe that **revolution** against Great Britain was the only answer.

Structured Vocabulary Discussion

When your teacher says a vocabulary word, have the people in your group take turns saying the first word they think of. Continue until your teacher says, "Stop." Then have the last person who said a word explain how his or her word is related to the vocabulary word.

Throughout the week, add to your vocabulary journal entries. Record new insights and other words that relate to this week's vocabulary.

Picture It

Copy this word organizer into your vocabulary journal. Fill in the sections with words that tell what happens in a **conflict**.

Copy this word web into your vocabulary journal. Fill in the circles with groups that have **representatives**.

people argue

conflict

Continental Congress

representatives

Make Connections

As you read, try to make connections between what you read and what you already know. Thinking about what you have heard or seen or done or read before will help you learn more from a story.

A **CONNECTION** is a link between two ideas.

To make a connection, relate new ideas in the text to what you already know.

TURN AND TALK Listen as your teacher reads these lines from *Dangerous Crossing*, in which Johnny and his father, John Adams, sail to France. They hope to gain assistance for the Americans in their war against Great Britain. With a partner, read the lines again and discuss the following questions.

- Have you ever done something that would help your family? Explain your answer.

- What have you heard, read, or seen about other persons who took chances for their family or for their country? Explain.

It was dangerous to cross the ocean in mid-winter, but time was pressing. The war with England, now almost three years old, was not going well. The rebel army had barely limped into their winter quarters. Many colonial soldiers lacked muskets and powder. They were also short of clothes, blankets, and shoes.

The new Americans desperately needed the support of other countries—especially France, England's greatest rival. Other representatives were in Paris already, but their progress was uncertain. It was hoped that the calm and thoughtful John Adams could do more.

In the Text

"The new Americans desperately needed the support of other countries—especially France, England's greatest rival."

This Reminds Me Of...

I know that sports teams have rival teams—teams that they try extra hard to beat. Countries can have rivals, too. If France was England's rival, then France might want to help the Americans in a war against England.

On Boston's FREEDOM TRAIL

by David L. Dreier

I like the old book *Johnny Tremain*. The book is about a boy in Boston during the American Revolution. Reading the book made me want to learn more about the Revolution. It also made me want to visit Boston. When I finally got to go there with my family, we headed straight for the Freedom Trail. The trail is a series of landmarks from the Colonial era and the early days of the nation. A 2.5-mile red brick line connects the places on the trail.

We followed the Freedom Trail on a pleasant fall day. The guidebooks start the tour at the Boston Commons. We started at the end of the trail and worked our way to the start. I stopped at the Bunker Hill Monument, which stands on the site of the first major battle of the American Revolution. I could almost smell the musket fire and hear the troops in battle as I read about the fighting.

Bunker Hill Monument

I thought about *Johnny Tremain* when we visited Paul Revere's house. In the book, Johnny's friend Rab died at the Battle of Lexington. Paul Revere risked his life to warn others that the British were headed toward Lexington and Concord. That took courage.

Near the end of our walk, we stopped at the Granary Burying Ground. The cemetery gets its name from the grain storage building (a granary) that once stood on the grounds. I visited Paul Revere's grave. I also visited the grave of John Hancock. John Hancock was the first person to sign the Declaration of Independence. As I stood at John Hancock's grave, I couldn't help thinking, "You and Paul Revere and the other Patriots did well, John. Rest in peace."

Paul Revere's House

Granary Burying Ground

Paul Revere captured (A.M.)

Lexington

④ Old North Bridge ⑤

South Bridge

③ Concord

M A S S A C H U S E T T S
Middlesex County

Mystic River

②

⑥
Charlestown

Boston

Cambridge ①

Back Bay

Charles River

N W E S

LEGEND

→ American attacks and advances
→ British advances
- -▸ British return to Charlestown

0   1   2   3mi

SCALE

❶ British troops leave Boston
❷ British troops clash with Americans at Lexington
❸ British troops arrive in Concord to search for supplies
❹ Americans challenge British troops
❺ Americans clash with British as British return to Boston
❻ British arrive back in Charlestown

GOOD CITIZENS OF BOSTON

Unite in Protest Against the Presence of British Troops

Since last fall, the British government has sent a growing number of troops to Boston. Nearly 4,000 redcoats now walk our streets. This is about one soldier for every four citizens! We, the good people of Boston, will not stand for this! Boston belongs to us!

Every day we hear stories of soldiers threatening our citizens. The soldiers stop us on the streets at night and demand to know where we are going. Off-duty soldiers take our jobs to earn extra money. This is wrong! These jobs belong to the people of Boston.

The British soldiers' tents crowd our Commons area. Now the British government expects us to house these soldiers in our homes! Let King George and the British government know that we will not stand for this abuse!

Short Vowels Review

Activity One

About Short Vowels

The letters *a, e, i, o,* and *u* are vowels. Say these short-vowel words aloud: *hat, hen, pig, dog, bun.* Notice that these sounds do not sound like the name of the letter. As your teacher reads *Good Citizens of Boston*, listen for the short-vowel sounds. Note that words with more than one syllable may contain more than one type of vowel sound.

Short Vowels in Context

With a partner, read *Good Citizens of Boston*. Write each short-vowel word you find in a chart like this one. Write the short vowel. Then think of another word with the same short-vowel sound.

WORD	VOWEL	WORD WITH THE SAME VOWEL SOUND
sent	e	bent

Activity Two

farming   bottle

better   muster

quick   pitter

Explore Words Together

The list on the right contains words with a short-vowel sound. With a partner, change each word to another short-vowel word by changing a vowel. For example, you can change the word *farming* into *forming*. List the new words and talk about them with a partner.

Activity Three

Explore Words Together

Choose three of the words that you made in the last activity. Write a sentence that uses each word and one *new* word with a short vowel.

THE NIGHTTIME RIDE OF Sybil Ludington

BY ELISE OLIVER

CAST OF CHARACTERS

Sybil, a 16-year-old girl

Rebecca, Sybil's 14-year-old sister

Archibald, Sybil's 10-year-old brother

Henry, Sybil's 8-year-old brother

Derrick, Sybil's 6-year-old brother

Colonel Ludington, the children's father

Mrs. Ludington, the children's mother

Narrator

ACT 1   SCENE 1

Setting: An empty stage. The narrator, dressed in clothing from the Revolutionary War, walks onto the stage.

NARRATOR: You've probably heard of Paul Revere. You may know Revere raced through the night to warn the Americans that the British were coming. But have you heard of Sybil Ludington? Sybil was a 16-year-old girl who went on her own nighttime ride. On April 26, 1777, British soldiers attacked a town in Connecticut. The men who made up the local American army were spread out across the countryside. Someone had to warn them. Sybil knew she was just the girl for the job!

Have you read about Paul Revere's ride in other sources? Explain.

ACT 1 SCENE 2

Setting: The Ludington household. Sybil and her family are sitting by the fire. It is dark and cold outside.

DERRICK: I want to hear a story before bedtime.

MRS. LUDINGTON: Why don't you tell us the story of your nighttime ride, Sybil?

SYBIL: *(embarrassed)* Oh, there's not much to tell.

COLONEL LUDINGTON: Come now, Sybil! You made us all proud that night. General Washington himself congratulated you on your bravery.

MRS. LUDINGTON: You definitely earned a bit of notice that night.

HENRY: Oh, please tell us about that night, Sybil!

SYBIL: *(smiling)* Oh, very well. Let's see . . . it all happened the night of April 26, 1777, during a terrible storm. Father had just come inside from working at the mill when there was a loud pounding on the front door.

REBECCA: I remember that! We all ran upstairs because the pounding frightened us so!

ARCHIBALD: Not all of us. Henry and I weren't scared a bit.

DERRICK: Who was at the door?

SYBIL: It was a messenger. Father needed to gather his soldiers at once!

> What other accounts have you read, seen, or heard about in which a person took risks to deliver a message?

COLONEL LUDINGTON: You see, two thousand redcoats had attacked Danbury!

DERRICK: What's a redcoat?

ARCHIBALD: A soldier in the British army. They wear bright red jackets, so we call them redcoats.

Read, Cover, Remember, Retell Technique With a partner, take turns reading as much text as you can cover with your hand. Then cover up what you read and retell the information to your partner.

COLONEL LUDINGTON: The redcoats were burning the storehouse. The army's weapons and food were being destroyed!

REBECCA: Our army would not be able to conquer the British without supplies.

SYBIL: Father needed to get all the local people to meet at our house and prepare them for battle.

COLONEL LUDINGTON: I needed a brave, fast rider to take this news to every farmhouse in the area.

ARCHIBALD: I should have been the one to ride! Not a girl!

REBECCA: *(shocked)* Archibald!

(Archibald stomps off stage)

Have you ever had to take action in an emergency? What happened?

COLONEL LUDINGTON: He's still upset that I didn't let him ride because of his fever.

MRS. LUDINGTON: It's getting late children. Sybil, you can finish your story another time.

(The room goes dark and the curtain falls.)

ACT 2 SCENE 1

(Setting: Mrs. Ludington and the children are sitting on the front porch of their home. It is a cool, sunny afternoon.)

REBECCA: Sybil, can you continue the story about your nighttime ride?

ARCHIBALD: Not that again. I'm tired of listening to it.

MRS. LUDINGTON: Oh, be nice, Archibald. Please continue your story, Sybil.

SYBIL: When I overheard Father talking to the messenger from Danbury, I knew I could help. I begged him to let me go, and he finally agreed, after making me promise I would be cautious. We saddled Star, and I rode as fast as I could. I didn't want to waste time getting on and off my horse to deliver the message, so I used a long stick to bang on the doors. I yelled over the thunder and rain, "The British are burning Danbury! Gather at the Ludingtons'!"

Have you ever had to deliver a message quickly to a lot of people? How did you do it?

HENRY: A long stick? That was an excellent idea, Sybil.

SYBIL: Thank you, Henry. I delivered the message to every soldier in Father's unit, and then I rode home as fast as I could. I have never been so happy to see our house!

(the curtain falls)

ACT 2   SCENE 2

Setting: An empty stage. The narrator, dressed in clothing from the Revolutionary War, walks out on the stage.

NARRATOR: Sybil traveled about 40 miles. She rode all through the night. Sybil and Star came home soaked to the skin and covered in mud from the road. But Sybil got the job done! Thanks to her help, Colonel Ludington's men were able to join up with other colonial soldiers and defeat the British in battle. News of Sybil Ludington's nighttime ride reached far and wide. General George Washington even thanked her.

What difficult job have you ever had to do? Describe your experience.

Think and Respond

Reflect and Write

- You and your partner took turns reading and retelling sections of *The Nighttime Ride of Sybil Ludington*. Discuss the sections you retold to each other.

- On one side of an index card, write down what you retold to your partner. On the other side, write down the connections you were able to make.

Short Vowels in Context

Reread *The Nighttime Ride of Sybil Ludington* to find examples of words containing short vowels. Have a contest with a partner to see who can find the most short-vowel words. Write down the words you find. Then write four sentences using some of the words you found. Share your favorite sentence with a partner.

Turn and Talk

MAKE CONNECTIONS

Discuss with a partner what you have learned so far about how to make connections.

- What does it mean to make connections?

- How do you make a connection?

- How does making connections help you understand what you read?

Choose one connection you made while reading *The Nighttime Ride of Sybil Ludington*. Explain that connection to a partner.

Critical Thinking

Discuss the events described in *The Nighttime Ride of Sybil Ludington*. In a group, write down the most important steps in Sybil's ride in the order they took place. Then answer these questions.

- Why was it difficult to gather the colonial soldiers together quickly?

- Why was Sybil a better choice than her father for the job of contacting the colonial soldiers?

Revolutionary War Time Line

1773

BOSTON TEA PARTY

Great Britain places **taxes** on tea shipped to America. On the night of December 16, a group of colonists dress as Native Americans and board tea ships in Boston Harbor. The men throw hundreds of chests of tea into the water in protest.

1774

FIRST CONTINENTAL CONGRESS

The British close the port of Boston. Alarmed, colonial leaders **assemble** in Philadelphia in 1774. The leaders hope to reason with the British. But reason fails. War breaks out.

1776

DECLARATION OF INDEPENDENCE

The Second Continental Congress adopts the Declaration of Independence.

1777

VALLEY FORGE

The war goes badly for the Americans at first. The winter at Valley Forge is very hard. The American soldiers are hungry, cold, and sick. The British may **defeat** the Americans.

1781

BATTLE OF YORKTOWN

After many battles, the tide has slowly turned for the Americans. Then, on October 19, a British army surrenders to George Washington at Yorktown. After this defeat, the British realize they cannot **conquer** the Americans.

1783

TREATY OF PARIS

The war officially ends. America now faces a new challenge. The young country must work for a strong **union** .

Structured Vocabulary Discussion

Work with a partner to complete the following sentences about your vocabulary words.

Conquer and **defeat** are *similar* because they both. . . .

Assemble and **union** are *different* because. . . .

Throughout the week, add to your vocabulary journal entries. Record new insights and other words that relate to this week's vocabulary.

Picture It

Copy this word web into your vocabulary journal. Fill in the circles with things you need to **assemble**.

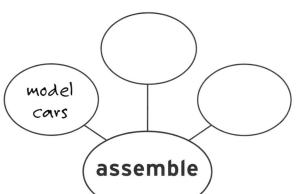

model cars

assemble

Copy this word organizer into your vocabulary journal. Fill in the boxes with things for which people pay **taxes**.

taxes
gasoline

March of the Redcoats

by Abby Jones

One match hissed, two lanterns lit

Two riders set out for Lexington

The faithful match, the rolling hooves

The only sounds that Boston heard

    While the British slipped 'cross the Charles

Meanwhile, the riders' news was told

With advising drums and alarming tales

One minute . . . two . . . More and more minutemen

Assemble for roll at Lexington

Too early for sunrise, a slice of Red

Swelled up from the fields and o'er the hill

A shot's been fired, a war's begun

Eight minutemen lay dead at Lexington, still—

    The British pressed on to Concord

The Redcoats marched 700 men

But all weren't there to hold the bridge

A full Redcoat retreat, the battle lost

Each tree hiding a Patriot's shots

    As the sun set early in Concord

A Letter to London from New York

January 1773

Dear Richard,

It was good to receive your last letter, my friend. You asked if I enjoy my new position with the hat maker. Yes, I am learning much about making hats the public wants to buy. Mr. Morton reminds me daily that the only good hat is a hat that sells.

Mr. Morton worries much about his business. He is fearful the King will put taxes on leather and cloth. Mr. Morton claims that higher taxes could seriously hurt business.

In your letter, you asked me how people in America feel about the actions of King George and his government. I must say, many of the people I see regularly are not happy. I think they hold views similar to those of Mr. Morton. The merchants I have met fear that King George might limit trade. Some also worry the King will force merchants to buy materials from a few suppliers. The situation is not good.

Your friend,

Jeremiah Reeves

Initial Consonants Review

Activity One

About Initial Consonants

The *g* in *gate* is an example of an initial consonant. As your teacher reads Jeremiah's letter, listen for initial consonants such as *g*, *m*, *p*, *f*, *r*, and *s*, at the beginnings of words.

Initial Consonants in Context

Make a list of the words in Jeremiah's letter that begin with *g*, *m*, *p*, *f*, *r*, or *s*. Next, pick one word for each consonant. Enter the word and its meaning in a chart like the one below.

INITIAL CONSONANT	WORD	MEANING
g	government	a group of people who rule or manage a country, state, district, or city

Activity Two

Explore Words Together

Look at the words to the right. Work together to see how many words you can make by adding the initial consonant *g*, *m*, *p*, *f*, *r*, or *s*. For example, consonants can be added to *-atter* to make *matter*, *patter*, and *fatter*.

-atter   -oat

-ellow   -unny

-utter

Activity Three

Explore Words in Writing

Write a short description of a place you would like to visit. In each sentence, include at least three words beginning with *g*, *m*, *p*, *f*, *r*, or *s*. Share your description with a partner.

WOMEN of the Revolution

by Alice Leonhardt

In the 1700s, girls generally learned to cook, sew, and read. Young women married, raised children, and listened to their husbands. Most husbands were in charge of the money and made important decisions. By law, women could not vote or join the army. Most women did not go to school. Yet, as the thirteen colonies fought for freedom from Great Britain, women played important roles.

Penelope Barker: Protester

Who She Was Penelope Barker was a wealthy North Carolina woman. Her husband, Thomas, was a port agent. This meant he collected taxes for the British government when ships unloaded their goods in port. The couple lived in Edenton, North Carolina.

What She Did Penelope Barker held a very special tea party in 1774. It was not your usual tea party. The guest list was long— 51 women! Barker didn't serve British tea at her party. Instead, she served a blend of raspberry leaves and mulberry plants. Barker urged her guests to stop buying British tea and cloth. Barker thought the British taxes on these goods were unfair. Barker was very convincing. Most of her guests signed a pledge saying they would not buy British goods.

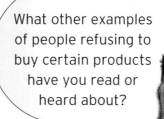
What other examples of people refusing to buy certain products have you read or heard about?

Mary Katherine Goddard: Reporter

Who She Was Mary Katherine Goddard ran a newspaper, the *Maryland Journal*. Goddard did everything. She gathered the news, wrote the stories, and ran the printing press. Goddard was also a printer. She printed the first copy of the Declaration of Independence that included the names of the signers.

What She Did Goddard reported on the war. The war was a hard time for newspapers. Paper was in short supply. But Goddard was able to keep her newspaper running. Many people relied on the *Journal* for news about the war.

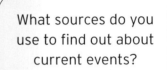

What sources do you use to find out about current events?

Phillis Wheatley: Poet

Who She Was Phillis Wheatley was a poet. She was also a slave. Luckily, the family she lived with encouraged Wheatley to write poetry. The young poet gained her freedom in 1773.

What She Did Wheatley's first poem was printed when she was only 14. In 1773, she published her first book of poetry. The young poet wrote many patriotic poems during the war. One of her best-known poems was about George Washington.

Lydia Darragh: Patriot Spy

Who She Was Lydia Darragh (DA-ra) was a wife and mother. She lived with her husband, William, and their children in Philadelphia. Her friends described her as a weak, delicate woman. Darragh may not have been strong, but she was brave.

Reverse Think-Aloud Technique Listen as your partner reads part of the text aloud. Choose a point in the text to stop your partner and ask what he or she is thinking about the text at that moment. Then switch roles with your partner.

What She Did In September 1777, British troops marched into Philadelphia. The troops took over many colonists' homes. The British let the Darraghs stay in their home. But they demanded that the family provide a meeting room for British officers. On the night of December 2, the British met to plan an attack on Washington's army. Lydia Darragh hid and listened. The next day, the brave woman said she needed to buy flour. While out, Darragh slipped a message to Washington's army warning of the attack. The British knew a spy had gotten word to Washington. But they did not know the spy was a woman!

What other true stories about spies have you seen on television or on film?

Deborah Sampson: Revolutionary Soldier

Who She Was Deborah Sampson was a tall, broad-shouldered woman from Massachusetts. As a girl, Sampson worked as a servant on a farm. She never went to school. Instead, Sampson got an education by reviewing the lessons of her employer's sons. When she grew up, Sampson taught school for several years.

What She Did During the war, many women helped their husbands and fathers on the battlefields. The women made bullets, loaded muskets, and brought food and water to the soldiers. By law, however, women could not join the army. That didn't stop Deborah Sampson! In May 1782, Sampson dressed as a man and joined the army. She used the name Robert Shurtliff. Sampson served for about a year and a half before the army discovered the truth. The army honorably discharged Sampson and sent her home. After the war, Sampson received land and a soldier's pension for her brave service.

Have you ever achieved a goal that other people didn't think you could accomplish? Explain.

Nanye'hi: Cherokee Peacemaker

Who She Was Nanye'hi (nan-YUH-hee) was a Cherokee. Some of her colonial friends called her Nancy Ward. Nanye'hi fought alongside her husband in battle against the Creek. The Creek killed her husband. But Nanye'hi kept fighting. In honor of her bravery, the tribe gave Nanye'hi the title "Beloved Woman." They also gave her a leadership role in the tribe.

What She Did The colonists sought the tribe's support in the Revolutionary War. So did the British. Each side promised something in return. The colonists promised a union of friendship and trade. The British promised to remove the colonists from the tribe's lands. Some of the tribe sided with the British. Nanye'hi sided with the colonists. She worked hard to keep the peace between the colonists and the Cherokee.

What happened when you tried to keep peace between two people who were ready to fight?

Think and Respond

Reflect and Write

- You and your partner took turns reading *Women of the Revolution* aloud. Discuss the thoughts and ideas you had as you read your sections.

- On one side of an index card, write one of the connections you made. On the back, explain that connection.

Initial Consonants in Context

Reread *Women of the Revolution* to find examples of words beginning with the consonants *g, m, p, f, r,* and *s*. Write down the words you find, and then share them with a partner. Work together to write a paragraph about women in the Revolution using the words you found.

Turn and Talk

MAKE CONNECTIONS

Discuss with a partner what you have learned so far about using background knowledge to make connections.

- What does it mean to make connections?

- How does making connections help you understand what you read?

Choose one connection you made while reading *Women of the Revolution*. Explain that connection to a partner.

Critical Thinking

In a small group, talk about the women described in *Women of the Revolution*. Pick one woman from the selection.

Write a summary of what that woman did in the Revolution. Then answer these questions.

- How did that woman's actions contribute to the Colonial cause?

- In what ways did that woman break away from the roles that most people expected women to play at that time?

THEME 2

Creating a New Nation

Contents

Modeled Reading

Shared Reading

Interactive Reading

Give Me Liberty!

The Story of the Declaration of Independence

by RUSSELL FREEDMAN

Strategic Listening

Strategic listening means listening to make sure you understand the selection. Listen to the focus questions your teacher will read to you.

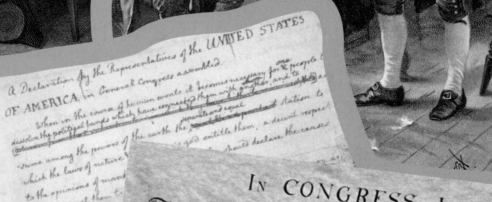

Independence!

Philadelphia, July 8, 1776

Dear John,

What an exciting day! There was a public reading outside the State House of a very important declaration . I wish you could have heard the bells ring. With this Declaration of Independence, the whole world will know that the United States is an independent country!

I had such a feeling of patriotism as I heard the document read. I've been lucky enough to play a small role in our country's decision to break free from Great Britain. For the last month, I've served as a clerk in the State House. I've watched the important debate over independence.

Last week was particularly interesting. Earlier, Mr. Thomas Jefferson had agreed to write the Declaration of Independence. Then the rest of the group, who called themselves Congress, spent part of last week going over his draft. They made quite a few changes. I don't think Mr. Jefferson was pleased. I saw Mr. Benjamin Franklin trying to cheer him up. Still, I'm sure that he was proud when the Congress approved the final version on July 4th.

Be sure to write and tell me all the details about the public reading in New York.

Your friend,

Zachary

Structured Vocabulary Discussion

When your teacher says a vocabulary word, you and your partner should each write down the first words you think of on a piece of paper. When your teacher says, "Stop," exchange papers with your partner and explain to each other any of the words on your lists.

Throughout the week, add to your vocabulary journal entries. Record new insights and other words that relate to this week's vocabulary.

Picture It

Copy this word organizer into your vocabulary journal. Fill in the ovals with words that describe **patriotism**, and list ways to show patriotism in the boxes.

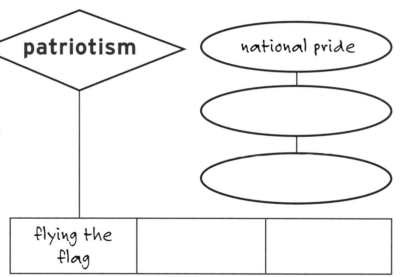

patriotism

national pride

flying the flag

Copy this word web into your vocabulary journal. Fill in the circles with examples of a **document**.

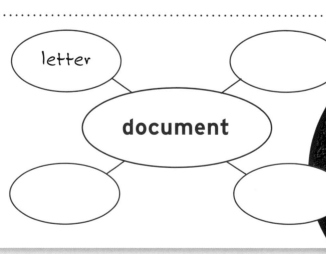

letter

document

When a bell is rung, people listen for something important.

Infer

When you infer, you combine what is in the text with your own knowledge to figure something out that is not directly stated in the text. Making inferences can help you learn more from a story.

When you INFER, you use your own ideas to better understand what you read.

Combine what you read and what you already know.

TURN AND TALK Listen as your teacher reads the following lines from *Give Me Liberty!* With a partner, reread the lines. Then discuss how you can combine what you know with what is stated in the text to infer something not directly stated. Discuss answers to the following questions with your partner.

• Why did Congress change the wording of Jefferson's draft?

• How do people working in large groups have to balance their views with the views of others?

Congress then turned to the wording of Jefferson's draft. During a three-day period, from late Tuesday, July 2, through Thursday, July 4, the delegates went over the document word by word. Jefferson, justly proud of his composition, squirmed in his seat, listening in unhappy silence as whole paragraphs were taken out, as new words and phrases were added. In all, nearly one hundred changes were made. Jefferson's text was cut by about a fourth. John Adams believed that Congress worked some real improvements into the text, but also "obliterated some of the best of it."

TAKE IT WITH YOU Making inferences helps you understand what you read. As you read other selections, try to use your own ideas and knowledge to discover more than what is directly stated in the text. Use a chart like the one below to infer.

In the Text		In My Head
"During a three-day period, from late Tuesday, July 2, through Thursday, July 4, the delegates went over the document word by word."	+	The delegates were very concerned that the Declaration say exactly what they wanted it to say.
"John Adams believed that Congress had worked some real improvements into the text, but had 'obliterated some of the best of it.'"	+	The Declaration of Independence was a very important document and many people made contributions to the final copy, even though Jefferson wrote it down first.

Gram's Declaration of Independence

by M. J. Cosson

Gram was moving to an apartment, and I wished she wouldn't. I loved her old house with its snug nooks and crannies, and especially its musty, old attic. But Gram was busy housecleaning, getting the place ready for sale. Gram said she wanted to sell because the upkeep of the house was too time-consuming.

I was in the attic sorting old papers for Gram. One by one, I went through stacks of storage boxes, throwing good stuff in one pile and junk in another. In one box, I came across a large sheet of paper that had the Declaration of Independence printed on it. The paper was yellow and brittle with age. An end was snipped off. I carelessly tossed it onto the "to keep" pile, thinking nothing of it.

That evening, as Dad and Gram looked around the attic, the Declaration caught Dad's eye. "Where is this document from?" he asked.

"Grandpa Fritz gave me that," Gram remembered.

"Perhaps we should have it appraised," Dad suggested. "This legend in the corner, 'W. J. Stone SC Washn.' might mean something important."

That night I searched the Internet. I learned that Thomas Jefferson wrote the draft of the Declaration. Then Congress adjusted the wording. Fifty-six men signed the final document. That was back in 1776.

The original Declaration was valuable. So, in 1820, the government asked that 200 copies be made. The printer later made some unofficial copies. The unofficial copies had the same legend as Gram's copy. When I read that, I got excited. "Dad!" I called out. "We'd better take Gram's Declaration of Independence to the museum."

The people at the museum called in a specialist. She said that Gram's document is probably one of the unofficial copies from the 1820s. Many unofficial copies were printed and sold to individuals, so most copies weren't worth much money.

When we returned home, I did more research about copies of the Declaration of Independence. I learned that some copies were elaborately decorated. Then I remembered my social studies project. More accurately, I remembered that I hadn't decided on a topic yet.

"Of course, you may use this copy as the centerpiece of your project," Gram replied when I asked to borrow her document. "It's wonderful that a forgotten piece of paper in my attic can help you learn more about independence!"

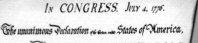

In CONGRESS. July 4, 1776.
The unanimous Declaration of the thirteen United States of America,

Freedom for All

July 1776

Dear Diary,

My family has awaited the Declaration of Independence with great hope. My parents were sure that it would include a strong statement against slavery. Father and others had pushed Congress to consider the issue. But it did not happen. The document makes no mention of the unjust practice. We are saddened. It was a glum time at dinner.

Father says that his friends in Congress claim Mr. Jefferson spoke against slavery in his draft. Mr. Adams supported him. But other members of Congress snuffed out the words. Father says that fear snatched victory from the foes of slavery. The cost was too high. Passage of the Declaration was the first aim. And passage required the southern colonies to cast YES votes. Many southern colonists support slavery.

Mother says not to give up hope. Americans love liberty. She believes the snare of slavery cannot hold such people forever. In time, Mother thinks most people will see that it is in everyone's best interest to end slavery. I trust this will happen soon.

Emma

Poet Phyllis Wheatley, 1753–1784

Consonant Blends
sn- and *-st*

Activity One

About Consonant Blends

When two consonants come together at the beginning or end of a word and you hear both sounds, the sounds you say together are called a consonant blend. For example, look at the beginning of the word *snap*. The sounds you say together for the letters *sn-* make up a consonant blend. As your teacher reads *Freedom for All*, listen carefully for the *sn-* and *-st* consonant blends.

Consonant Blends in Context

With a partner, read *Freedom for All*. Find words with *sn-* and *-st*. Write the words in a chart like the one below. Choose one word from each list and write a sentence that shows its meaning.

CONSONANT BLEND	WORDS	SENTENCE
sn-	snuffed	Mother snuffed out the candle with her fingers.
-st	against	It was difficult to walk against the wind.

Activity Two

Explore Words Together

Look at the list of words on the right. Work with a partner to change either the beginning or end sound of each word by using the consonant blend *sn-* or *-st*. For example, change the *-d* in *toad* to *-st* to make the new word *toast*.

toad	match
share	wring
thrush	plug

Activity Three

Explore Words in Writing

Choose four of the new words in Activity Two. Write a sentence for each new word. Share your sentences with a partner.

The Declaration of Independence

Thomas Jefferson's Reflections
retold by Alice McGinty

*The following selection is written in the style of a memoir.
It is based on Thomas Jefferson's autobiography.*

In 1769, I became a member of the colonial legislature in Virginia. I continued as a member until the revolution closed down the legislature. While a member, I made one effort to free the slaves. I was not surprised when the effort failed. At the time, we believed our first duty was to protect the interests of England. This closed our minds to many good ideas. England made money from the slave trade. Thus, I could not really expect to succeed. However, experience soon proved that our inability to take action was a matter of habit and despair. It was not a matter of belief and will. We could do the right thing when given the chance.

Relations with the British got worse. Some of us set up a voluntary convention to consider actions. We knew it was urgent that each colony view an attack on one colony to be an attack on the whole group of colonies. The first step was to set up committees to correspond between the colonies. This would allow us to share information. The next step was to call for a meeting in a central place. Each colony would send delegates to plan a common course of action. Finally, the call came. We were to meet in Philadelphia!

What sort of actions were the colonists considering at this time?

We named this meeting the First Continental Congress. It began on September 5, 1774. When it ended on October 26, members agreed to meet again in May, 1775. I joined this Second Continental Congress in June, 1775. One of my tasks was to help prepare a paper. The paper outlined reasons for taking up arms against the British. Some thought my views too strong. The Congress wanted to move against the king with care. The final paper contained few of my views.

Then, on May 15, 1776, the Virginia convention announced a plan to the delegates in Congress. The Virginia convention wanted to declare the colonies independent of Great Britain, draft a declaration of their rights, and form a new government to bond the colonies. On June 7th, Congress met to debate the issues.

Again, Congress called for caution. Some colonies were not yet ready to fall from the parent stem of Britain. We thought it best to wait for them. Those colonies would come around. We put off a decision until July 1st.

> Why do you think some people in Congress wanted to move against the king with care?

Public reading of the Declaration of Independence

Jefferson's Notecards

Say Something Technique Take turns reading a section of text, covering it up, and then saying something about it to your partner. You may say any thought or idea that the text brings to your mind.

Still, we felt there should be as little delay as possible. Therefore, Congress chose a committee to write a Declaration of Independence. I served on the committee. So did John Adams, Dr. Franklin, Roger Sherman, and Robert R. Livingston. The committee requested I do the writing. I agreed to take on the task. We submitted the Declaration to Congress on Friday the 28th of June. Congress read the Declaration. But they took no action.

Why do you think the committees started work on the Declaration of Independence even though Congress was still debating?

On Monday, Congress once again turned its attention to Virginia's call for independence. Again, we did not have the votes. But this time, one person had confidence that he could change a few minds. Congress agreed to hold off voting until Tuesday, July 2. On Tuesday, several factors were in our favor. First, a few new delegates were in attendance. These people

Assembly Room of Independence Hall

turned their colonies' votes from *no* to *yes*. Second, New York withdrew from the vote, saying that it did not have orders from home. Thus, when the delegates cast their votes, twelve colonies gave their voice for independence. Several days later, New York added its *yes* vote.

Thomas Jefferson reading the rough draft of the Declaration of Independence to Benjamin Franklin

Congress now considered the Declaration of Independence. The debates took the greater parts of the 2nd, 3rd, and 4th days of July and proceeded at a snail's pace. Congress made many changes. The cowardly idea that we still had friends in England worth keeping haunted many people's minds. For this reason, Congress struck out those passages that might offend the people of England. Congress also snipped out the clause disapproving of slavery. They did this to please South Carolina and Georgia. Both wished to continue importing slaves. Then, there were our neighbors to the north. I believe they also felt a little sensitive about slavery. Their people have very few slaves. But they carry slaves for others.

Based on this memoir, how do you think Jefferson felt about slavery?

During the debate over the Declaration, I was sitting by Dr. Franklin. He observed that I was squirming a little with the changes to my work. I suppose I was. I believe that you can know the thoughts and feelings of a person not only by what they accept, but also by what they reject.

The debates closed on the evening of July 4th. Congress agreed to the wording. All but one member present signed the document. Someone then copied the words onto parchment. The delegates signed this copy on the 2nd of August.

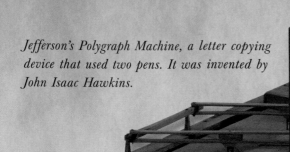
Jefferson's Polygraph Machine, a letter copying device that used two pens. It was invented by John Isaac Hawkins.

Congress's changes deeply troubled Thomas Jefferson. He was so upset that he took the time to create hand copies of his original words and mark the changes that Congress made. Jefferson sent these copies to a few close friends. Richard Henry Lee was one of those friends. Lee shared Jefferson's unhappiness. In the letter below, he tells his friend that he wishes Congress had not "mangled" the words. But Lee also offers comfort, saying, "no Cookery can spoil the Dish." In other words, Congress's editing cannot ruin Jefferson's ideas.

Chantilly, 21st. July 1776

Dear Sir,

Thank you much for your favor and its enclosures by this post, and I wish sincerely, as well for the honor of Congress, as for that of the States, that the Manuscript had not been mangled as it is. It is wonderful, and passing pitiful, that the rage of change should be so unhappily applied. However, the Thing is in its nature so good, that no Cookery can spoil the Dish for the palates of Freemen. . . .

Richard Henry Lee

Why do you think Thomas Jefferson sent his friends copies of the original Declaration of Independence showing the edits made by Congress?

Think and Respond

Reflect and Write

• You and your partner read sections of *The Declaration of Independence* and said something about the text. Discuss your thoughts and ideas.

• Choose two inferences you made while you read the memoir and write them on index cards. On the back of each index card, write what information in the text allowed you to make the inference.

Consonant Blends in Context

As you reread *The Declaration of Independence*, write examples of words with the consonant blends *sn-* and *-st*. Then write three sentences that describe how you feel about the Declaration of Independence. Be sure to include at least one word with *sn-* or *-st* in each sentence. Share your favorite sentence with a partner.

Turn and Talk

INFER

Discuss with a partner what you have learned so far about how to infer, or to make inferences.

• What is inferring? How do you infer?

• How does inferring help you better understand what you read?

Choose one inference you made while reading *The Declaration of Independence*. Explain that inference to a partner.

Critical Thinking

In a group, discuss the purpose of the Declaration of Independence and its role in creating the new nation. Then write answers to these questions.

Jefferson's Revolving Book Stand

• Why do you think Congress thought it was important to have a Declaration of Independence?

• Why do you think Thomas Jefferson was concerned about the changes Congress made to the Declaration?

• Why do you think Congress though it was important to change some of Thomas Jefferson's words?

Spreading the Word

Hear Ye! Hear Ye! Congress wanted people to support independence. For that, they needed the public's **confidence**. People had to know that Congress had acted with caution. Leaders of the **Convention** thought the Declaration of Independence would do that. They hurried to get out the word.

Spread the Word

Congress drafted a letter ordering that cities and towns **proclaim** the Declaration. Printers quickly made copies of the Declaration. Swift riders carried the copies across the land. Some places held ceremonies where they read the document to the people. Other places published the document in the newspaper. Some hung copies on buildings. All of the methods had the same aim—to build **allegiance** to the cause.

The Biggest Pep Rally of Them All!

The Declaration of Independence proclaimed the birth of a new **nation**. Many cities and towns held public celebrations. People rang bells, lit bonfires, put candles in the windows, and held parades. In many places, people tore down symbols of King George.

confidence convention proclaim nation allegiance

Structured Vocabulary Discussion

Work with a partner or in a small group to fill in the following blanks. Be sure you can explain how the words are related.

Student is to *school* as *delegate* is to _______.

State is to *county* as _______ is to *state*.

Throughout the week, add to your vocabulary journal entries. Record new insights and other words that relate to this week's vocabulary.

Picture It

Copy this word wheel into your vocabulary journal. Fill in the sections with names of things people can **proclaim**.

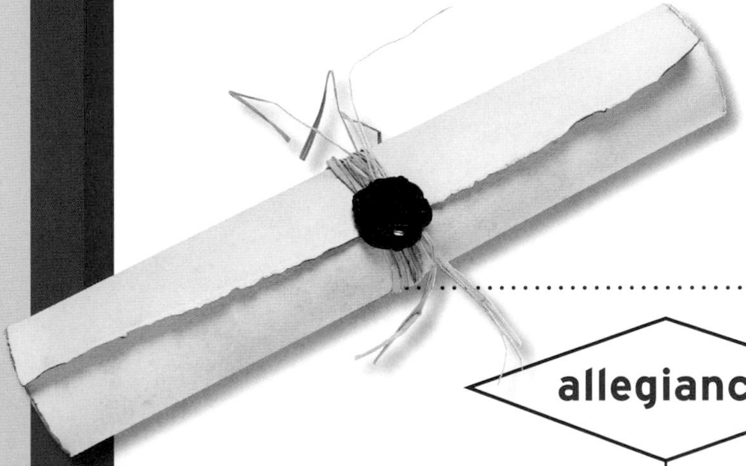

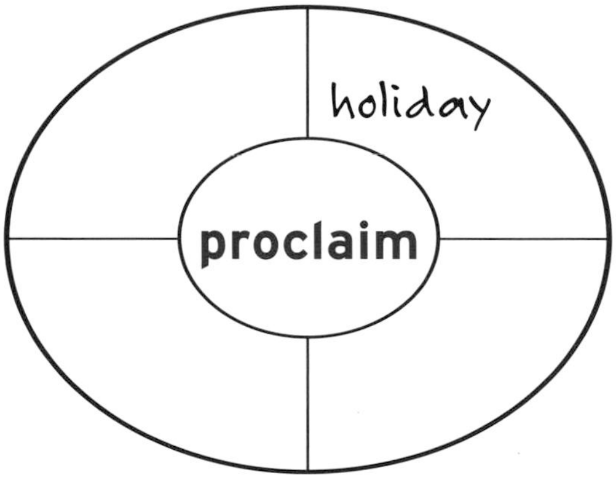

holiday
proclaim

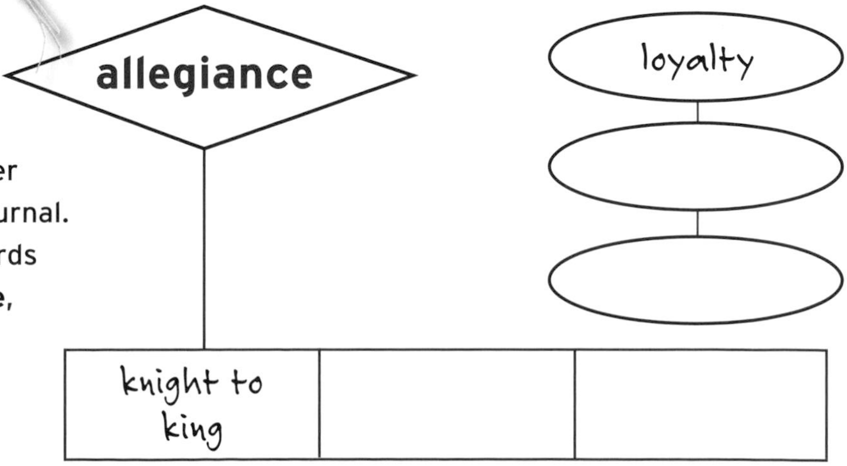

allegiance
loyalty
knight to king

Copy this word organizer into your vocabulary journal. Fill in the ovals with words that describe **allegiance**, and list examples of allegiance in the boxes.

Independence Day

by John Manos

The fun begins with blaring horns, with rattling drums and trilling fifes.

A marching band steps in formation

And floats roll past our viewing station—

We stand to watch our flag go by.

The afternoon gets warmer, and our picnic treats are packed in ice.

My gladness needs no explanation—

It's hot outside—I love vacation!

I love the lazy buzzing flies.

We sit on blankets near the lake as day turns slowly into night.

We pass the time in conversation,

And no one needs a reservation

To watch as fireworks spark the sky.

As darkness falls, the rockets rise with hissing whistles to the sky.

We strain to find the elevation

Of the missile's high location,

When, with a BLAST, flames fill our eyes.

And when the crashing show is over, we walk home with happy sighs—

A lovely day of celebration

For the birth of our great nation—

America—the Fourth of July!

LIBERTY!

On July 9, 1776, General George Washington called the Continental Army together for a reading of the Declaration of Independence. He looked out over a map of different, ragtag outfits. Almost every unit wore a different color. There was also a big gap in the quality of the dress. A lot of men lacked any uniform. Some men had no shoes or hats. Few looked like they fit together as an army.

The troops also lacked a common flag. Commanders needed a way to rally their troops to a specific spot. Flags usually served that function. General Washington knew that he would regret doing nothing, but to get the troops to agree on a common flag would not be easy.

Charles Lee, a general under Washington's command, came up with a temporary solution. All troops would rig up a big flag labeled with the word *LIBERTY*. *Liberty* was a word most people could accept. Like the men's dress, no two flags looked alike. But most did carry the word *Liberty*.

Actor for Revolutionary War Scene

Using Word Families

Activity One

About the Word Families

A word family is made up of words that end with the same vowel and consonant sound. For example, the *-ap* word family includes *map*, *lap*, *clap*, *unwrap* as well as many other words. As your teacher reads *LIBERTY!* listen for words in the same word families.

Word Families in Context

With a partner, read *LIBERTY!* First, find words in the article that belong to the same word family. List the words in a chart like the one below. Note that not all word families are represented in *LIBERTY!* Then, you and your partner fill in the chart with word families of your own.

WORD FAMILY	-ap	-et	-ig	-op	-ug	-at	-en	-it	-ot	-un
WORDS	map gap									

Activity Two

Explore Words Together

Look at the list of words on the right. Work with a partner to write other words that belong to each word family. Read aloud the new words you make.

mat	prop
burden	stun
grit	jug

Activity Three

Explore Words in Writing

You may have noticed that the words in each word family rhyme! Use words from one word family to write a rhyming poem. Share your poem with a partner.

A Tri-Corner Hat

A Statue Comes DOWN

by Melissa Blackwell Burke

The Declaration of Independence sent a message to King George. It shouted that the colonies were breaking free. But the document was also a symbol for the colonists. It stood for the right of people to seek liberty and freedom. The members of Congress knew this. That is one reason they ordered the document read in cities and towns throughout the colonies. The owner of a New York newspaper also knew it. He urged his readers to hang the Declaration in their houses for all to see.

But the Declaration was not the only symbol for the colonists. All around there were symbols of the king's power. In New York City on July 9, 1776, the colonists attacked one of these symbols. The characters in the following story are not real. But the events are. As you read, think about why the people might have done what they did.

What else have you read about this period in American history?

I've been a silversmith's apprentice for about a year, since the day I turned nine years old. I'm learning the trade of working with silver. In the shop where I work, we usually make teapots, bowls, plates, and utensils. I mostly assist the silversmith, but I have made a few simple things all on my own.

A few weeks ago, the silversmith had calls to make candleholders. Some people wanted to burn candles in their windows to celebrate the birthday of King George III. How things can change in a short time! Now many candles burn in windows, but it is to celebrate that King George no longer rules over us.

We learned this fact on July 9. General Washington called his men together. He read them the Declaration of Independence and explained that the thirteen colonies would proclaim their independence from Britain. We would form our own United States of America. I hear that the men applauded when they learned this. They shouted for joy. Then the news started spreading throughout New York City.

Have you ever seen a house with signs or decorations to show support for a cause? Explain.

Reverse Think Aloud Technique

Listen as your partner reads part of the text aloud. Choose a point in the text to stop your partner and ask what he or she is thinking about the text at that moment. Then switch roles with your partner.

In the silversmith shop, we were setting about our work and had no idea what was happening in the rest of the city. Then we heard bells ringing and knew that something important was taking place. The barrel maker from down the street ran in to tell us the news. "A crowd is gathering in Bowling Green Park," he said, and urged us to join him. The silversmith announced that we should go at once.

What movie or television program have you seen about the military struggle of the Americans against the British?

On the way to Bowling Green, I listened as the barrel maker and the silversmith talked about what was sure to come. The king would not give up easily. There would be more fighting, perhaps even in our own city. The barrel maker asked the silversmith whether he would fight. "If I am called to stand up for America, I will gladly lend my support," he said. "The states have my full allegiance."

We heard the shouts of "Independence! Independence!" well before we got to Bowling Green. As we drew closer, we saw a crowd gathered around the big golden statue of King George III. A man was standing next to the statue, addressing the crowd. We heard people clap and pat each other on the back.

We couldn't hear exactly what people were saying, but the silversmith had an idea. "People will no longer want to see a golden image of the king," he said. "They will not stand in the shadow of King George, who refused to rule a free people. Since there is no place for a king in America, I bet they will bring that statue down."

What other moments in which people rebelled against an unjust ruler have you heard or read about?

People from the crowd did indeed run forward toward the statue. I thought about how the statue had been there for as long as I could remember and what it meant that the people did not want to see it any more. They pulled the statue down, and then smashed it apart.

After a while, the silversmith, the barrel maker, and I made our way back to our shops. The news was spreading like a fire through the city. It set off celebrations everywhere. People were cheering in the streets. Some colonists were tearing down signs and pictures—anything that had to do with Britain and the king. The silversmith said these were ways to show that the new, independent America would be truly separate from the old colonies. As we got back to the shop, we heard someone firing musket shots. There were exactly thirteen shots, one for each of the 13 states.

We tried to settle back into our work, but it was a bit difficult with all the commotion. I thought about what I had seen and heard that day. I knew that those things meant both the end of something and the beginning of something new.

Have you ever had to settle back into a familiar routine after an exciting event? What happened?

Think and Respond

Reflect and Write

- You and your partner took turns reading parts of the text and asking each other what you thought about the text. Discuss the thoughts you shared and explain how they related to the text.

- On one side of an index card, write a connection you made between *A Statue Comes Down* and your own life or other things you have read, heard, or seen. On the other side, explain how that connection helped you understand the story.

Word Families in Context

Reread *A Statue Comes Down* to find examples of words in the same word families. Write down the words you find. Then use some of the words from the word to create a poem that describe the events in New York City on July 9, 1776. Share your poem with a partner.

Turn and Talk

MAKE CONNECTIONS

Discuss with a partner what you have learned about how to make connections.

- What are some ways you can make connections while you read?

- How does making connections help you understand what you are reading?

Choose one connection you made while reading *A Statue Comes Down*. Explain that connection to a partner.

Critical Thinking

In a group, review the events in *A Statue Comes Down*. Write the events in order. Then answer these questions.

- How did candleholders change from being symbols of loyal British citizens to symbols of resistance to the British?

- Why did the Americans pull down the statue of King George?

- What other symbolic acts take place in the story?

Serious Sound, 2005

Gil Mayers (1927–present)

THEME **3** **How Does Cooking Work?**

THEME **4** **What is Sound?**

Viewing

The artist who created this piece of art, called a *collage*, is Gil Mayers. A collage is made my putting together pieces of paper, cloth, photographs, or other materials. For his pictures, Mayers often combines depictions of people with brightly colored shapes. Many of the artist's works portray jazz musicians. Jazz is a 20th century American music, noted for its offbeat rhythms and sounds.

1. What parts of the picture show real things? What parts of the picture represent things that cannot be seen?

2. How do you think the process of creating a collage is similar to the process of cooking?

3. What do you think the artist meant by titling the picture *Serious Sound*?

In This UNIT

In this unit, you will think like a scientist. You will learn how stovetops and ovens transfer heat during cooking. You will also explore how vibrations produce many kinds of sound.

Contents

CHATO'S KITCHEN

by Gary Soto • illustrated by Susan Guevara

Critical Listening

Critical listening means listening for words that show emotion. Listen to the focus questions your teacher will read to you.

Recipe Notes

Dear Diary,

What a day! I had hoped that my first night as the new chef at The Good Egg would go well, but I did not expect to invent a wonderful new recipe by accident. When I arrived, I checked to make sure I had all the **ingredients** I would need. I decided to make the dessert first, so I whipped up some egg whites to make meringue cookies. I turned on the oven to preheat, but I did not feel any heat **radiation**. This could be a disaster. How was I going to prepare dinner and dessert for a restaurant full of people without a working oven?

Then I saw that the oven was unplugged. All I had to do was **connect** the oven to the power outlet. My staff **reassured** me that all would go well. However, I did not see the tray of melted chocolate above the oven. As I began to **transfer** the hot meringues from the oven, I accidentally bumped the tray. The melted chocolate spilled all over the meringues. What a mess! But the chocolate-covered meringues were the most popular dessert that night!

Ann

Structured Vocabulary Discussion

Work with a partner or in a small group to fill in the following blanks. Be sure you can explain how the words are related.

Find is to *discover* as *join* is to _____ .

Parts are to *bicycle* as _____ are to *bread*.

> Throughout the week, add to your vocabulary journal entries. Record new insights and other words that relate to this week's vocabulary.

Picture It

Copy this word organizer into your vocabulary journal. Fill in the ovals with words that mean **transfer**, and list examples of ways you can transfer something in the boxes.

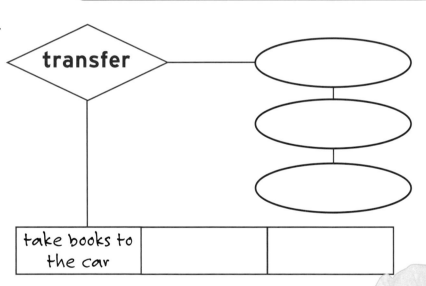

Copy this word wheel into your vocabulary journal. Name things that would make you feel **reassured** during a fire.

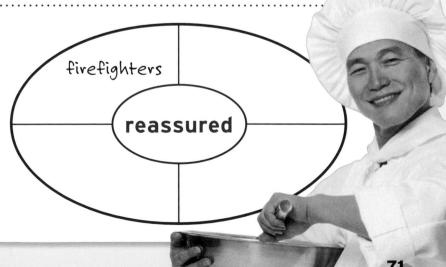

Ask Questions

Asking questions keeps you thinking about your reading. Asking questions before you read will help you to make predictions about what you are going to read. Asking questions during and after your reading will help you to understand the material better.

What **QUESTIONS** do you have about what you read?

Think about the questions you have in your mind as you read.

TURN AND TALK Listen as your teacher reads the following lines from *Chato's Kitchen*. Then with a partner, discuss answers to the following questions.

• What questions did you have when you heard the title *Chato's Kitchen*?

• What questions can you ask after listening to the passage?

Chorizo wagged into the house, his belly bumping over the threshold. He click-clicked on paw-nails into the kitchen, his nose picking up the smells of simmering food. He shivered the mice from his back, and they dropped like gray fruit.

"¡Hola!" Chorizo barked politely.

Chato and Novio Boy scampered from under the table and leaped up on the curtains, where they meowed for their lives.

"What are you doing there?" Mami mouse asked. "Don't tell me you're scared of Chorizo. *Mira*, he's a nice dog." Chorizo wagged his tail and let his tongue fall out.

TAKE IT WITH YOU You will have a better understanding of your reading if you ask questions about the text. Try to ask questions before, during, and after you read. As you read other selections, use a chart like the one below to help you create your own questions.

In the Text	"I Wonder" Question
"Chato's Kitchen"	I wonder: Who is Chato?
"He shivered the mice from his back, and they dropped like gray fruit."	I wonder: How did Chorizo and the mice become such good friends?
"Chato and Novio Boy scampered from under the table and leaped up on the curtains, where they meowed for their lives. 'What are you doing up there?' Mami mouse asked. 'Don't tell me you're scared of Chorizo. Mira, he's a nice dog.'"	I wonder: Will Chato and Novio Boy become friends with the mice and Chorizo?

Bake Your Own Bread

by Renée Carver

Nothing smells quite as appetizing as freshly baked bread. Here are recipes for two delicious kinds of bread that you can make with the help of an adult. One recipe is without yeast (which makes a flat, cracker-like bread), the other is with yeast (which makes a loaf of bread).

Golden Discs

What You Will Need

large bowl

mixing spoon

wooden cutting board

cookie sheet

rolling pin

4 cups of unbleached flour

1 teaspoon of salt

$1\frac{1}{2}$ cups of room temperature water

What You Will Do

1. Mix the flour and water together in a large bowl. If the dough is sticking to the sides of the bowl, add more water until all the dough can be shaped into a ball.

2. Sprinkle some flour on the wooden cutting board. Then knead the ball for 10 minutes.

3. Split the ball in half. Then split each half into 8 pieces and roll the dough bits between your palms to form 16 little balls.

4. Roll each ball out with your rolling pin until it is about 7 inches in diameter.

5. Lay the flat circles of dough on your cookie sheet and bake them in a preheated 500-degree oven for about 5 minutes or until they turn slightly brown and crisp.

White Bread

What You Will Need

2 large bowls

mixing spoon

cloth

2 9 × 5-inch loaf pans

2 cups of warm water

$\frac{2}{3}$ cup of white sugar

$1\frac{1}{2}$ tablespoons of active dry yeast

$\frac{1}{4}$ cup of vegetable oil

6 cups of bread flour

What You Will Do

1. Dissolve the sugar in the warm water and then stir in the yeast. Because yeasts are living, one-celled fungi, make sure the water is not too hot or it will kill the yeast cells. The mixture will foam as the yeast cells make carbon dioxide and ethanol bubbles. These bubbles cause the dough to rise.

2. Add the salt and oil to the warm-water mixture, and mix in the flour cup by cup.

3. Knead the dough, then coat the dough with oil and place it in the second bowl.

4. Cover the dough with a dampened cloth. Wait approximately an hour until the bubbles have caused the dough to rise to about twice its original size.

5. Knead the dough for five more minutes. Split it between the two baking pans. Let the dough rise for an additional 30 minutes, and then bake it for 30 minutes at 350 degrees.

Yeast-Free Bread vs. Yeast Bread

Golden Discs

yeast-, oil-, and sugar-free

can be baked immediately

baked for 5 minutes in 500° oven

hard and crispy

both

made from water, flour, and salt

dough is kneaded

baked in oven

White Bread

made with yeast, oil, and sugar

needs time to rise

baked for 30 minutes in a 350° oven

soft and fluffy

Max's Folly

Subject: Baked Alaska
Date: Thursday, July 6, 2006 11:21 AM
From: Max
To: Mike

Hi, Mike,

Baked Alaska—it looked so easy when you made one the last time you were home from college. Ice cream, meringue, and cake—how simple can it get? Let me tell you, the peaky white stuff is tricky, cake batter and meringue are extremely hard to get off the walls, and heat and ice cream don't mix!

My first mistake was to ignore the perfectly fine layer cake Mom had in the freezer. I decided to make the cake myself. All was going well until I turned on the mixer before I lowered the beaters. Cake batter flew everywhere! I decided I would be smart with the meringue—I'd use the blender. Well, now I know that if you take the lid off a blender while it's running, things fly almost as far as with a mixer.

Then there is the oven issue. Take my advice, when a recipe says bake in a hot oven for 6 to 7 minutes, you bake for only 6 or 7 minutes. When I finally opened the oven door, I had a very messy puddle of ice cream. It's a good thing we have a self-cleaning oven!

Your very tired brother,

Max ☹

Long Vowels Review

About Long Vowels

Some words end with a vowel, a consonant, and a silent *e*. The silent *e* at the end of the word causes the long-vowel sound. As your teacher reads *Max's Folly*, listen for the long-vowel sounds followed by a consonant. Which of these words ends with a silent *e*?

Long Vowels in Context

With a partner, read *Max's Folly* to find words with long-vowel sounds followed by a consonant and a silent *e*. Enter each word you find in a chart like the one below. Indicate the long-vowel pattern. Then think of another rhyming word for the long-vowel sound.

WORD	LONG-VOWEL SOUND	RHYMING WORD
made	ade	shade

Activity Two

Explore Words Together

With a partner, underline the long vowel and circle the silent *e* in the words on the right. Then change the word to another long-vowel word by changing one or more of the consonants. For example, you can make the word *code* into *rode* or *vote* by changing the consonants.

slice	hide
mole	code
rule	fume

Activity Three

Explore Words in Writing

Choose five of the words with the long-vowel, consonant, silent *e* pattern that you created. Write a sentence using each of the words. Share your favorite sentences with a partner.

Abuela's *Feast*

by Eileen Joyce

"**G**abriel and Manolo, I'm happy that you can spend the day with me," said Grandmother Gomez. Hugging the boys, she added, "I don't see enough of my grandsons now that you are growing up. I know that boys in the fifth grade always have a place to go and something to do. I'm pleased that today you will help your abuela."

"What kind of chores can I do to help you, Abuela?" asked Gabriel. "I can mow the lawn, edge the flower beds, or help in the garden before my baseball game."

"Today I have something different in mind. We'll begin to prepare food for the Cinco de Mayo party on May 5," she answered. "That is the day Mexico won a victory over the French army. To get ready for the party, I will need both of you to help in the kitchen with the food."

What questions do you have about Cinco de Mayo?

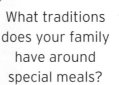

"Abuela, it's great to be here," said Manolo, smiling. "Gabriel and I don't get to spend much time together now that we go to different schools. It's always fun to get together and spend the day with you."

"Yes, this will be fun. I'll get some supplies from the pantry while you put on aprons," Abuela said leaving the room.

"I didn't know we would have to stay inside and cook all day," Gabriel grumbled under his breath. "I need to go to my baseball game, and I don't even like to cook."

Abuela came back to the kitchen carrying supplies. "We'll start with a special food, sweet tamales, made with raisins and pineapple."

"Oh, I know the tradition that goes with these tamales!' said Manolo. "We put a surprise in the bread we bake, and the one who finds the surprise has to pay for the tamales."

What traditions does your family have around special meals?

"That's right," replied Abuela.

"Doesn't it take *forever* to make tamales?" Gabriel asked, trying not to look distressed.

"Yes," Abuela agreed, "making tamales does have quite a few steps. It can take three people a couple of days to get everything ready."

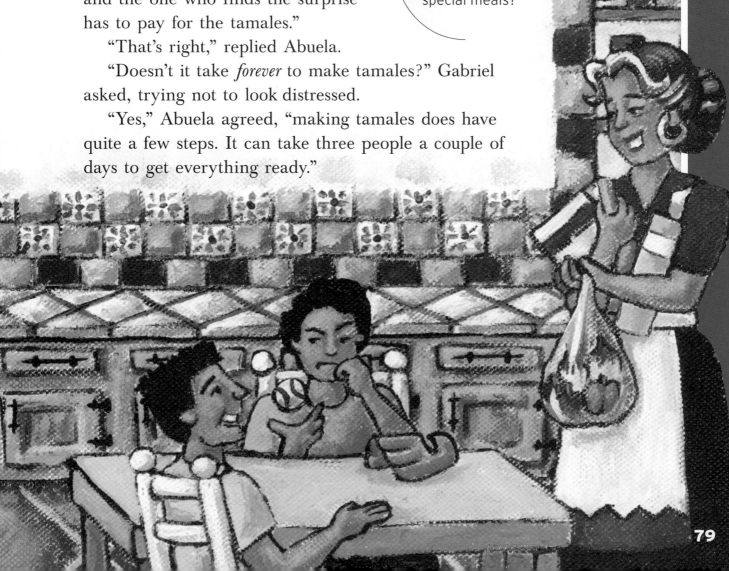

Reverse Think-Aloud Technique

Listen as your partner reads part of the text aloud. Choose a point in the text to stop your partner and ask what he or she is thinking about the text at that moment. Then switch roles with your partner.

"I almost forgot that I need to plan my science project today," Gabriel gulped.

"What's your topic, Gabriel?" asked Manolo.

"We're studying chemical reactions right now. What are you guys studying?"

"We're studying heat transfer." Gabriel mumbled. "I'm still deciding on a topic."

"We've already done heat transfer. I think I know how you can research your project and help Abuela cook at the same time," said Manolo. "Abuela, what other recipes will we fix for the party, and how will you cook the recipes?"

"I need different appliances for different things. For the empanadas, I'll use my new convection oven," she said. "I'll bake one pan of chicken enchiladas and one of cheese in the regular oven. I'll steam tamales on the stove, and I'll also use the microwave to heat soup."

"You're in luck, Gabriel. That menu provides the raw ingredients for a perfect science project! The cooking uses three types of heat transfer. You can start with a chart that defines the terms," Manolo said. "Then, you can fit in recipes, pictures of the food, and the type of appliance you used."

What questions do you have about the types of cooking Manolo mentions?

CONVECTION

CONDUCTION

MICROWAVE

"I know a little bit about convection ovens. We talked about them in class. A fan in a convection oven moves hot air around inside the oven. Moving air cooks food faster and at lower temperatures than plain hot air because the heat transfers more evenly. It can also get to all sides of the food. This makes food brown evenly," said Manolo.

"That's why Abuela wants to use the convection oven for the empanadas. The crust will be crisp, flaky, and brown all over," Gabriel said. "The pies will also cook fast and at a lower temperature. That means the kitchen won't get so hot. Convection must be the first type of heat transfer, but what's the second type?"

What questions do you have about how food is cooked?

"The second type of heat transfer is conduction. I remember the definition from the test. It's the direct movement of heat from one item to another. That's how a regular gas or electric oven and stovetop transfer heat. Gas or electricity heats a pan and the heat in the pan cooks the food. There's no fan. My teacher said it's best to put the pans on only one shelf so the food will brown evenly."

"Very good, Manolo. I know a few things, too. When the tamales are put together, I'll steam them on top of the stove," said Abuela. "The steam stores energy and then releases the heat into the food."

"Steaming must use conduction since it uses a pan, steam, and food. My science teacher would like this. We're putting scientific information to use," Gabriel smiled proudly. "Is that all the food we are going to have and all the cooking we'll be doing, Abuela?"

What questions do you have about the science of cooking based on the information on this page?

"Your families will bring hot sauce, tortillas, and tacos. I made Manolo's father's favorite soup," she said. "I use meat, vegetables, hominy, and spice. Before the party, we will reheat the soup in the microwave."

"The microwave is the third way of transferring heat. It uses radiation, a wave that sends energy through space. This process is the fastest way of heating food," Manolo said.

"I'm going to get my camera before we start cooking," Gabriel said. "I'll take pictures of the food ready to cook, cooking, and on platters and in bowls. This project will really impress my science teacher—and make him hungry!"

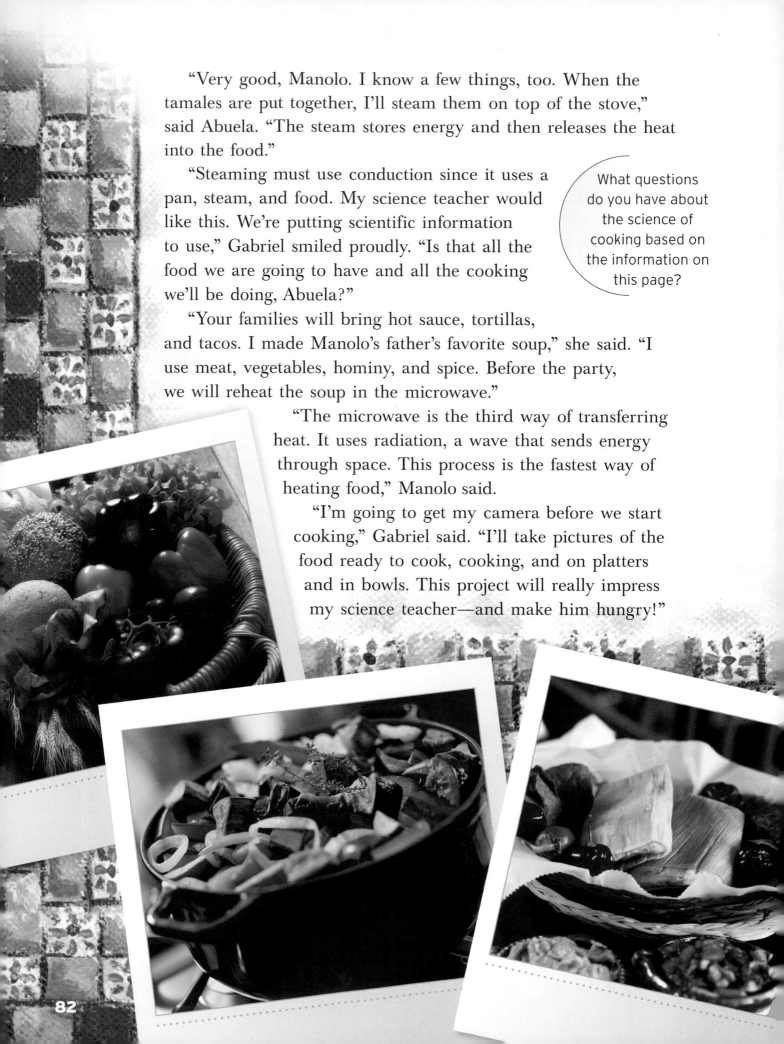

Think and Respond

Reflect and Write

• You and your partner took turns reading *Abuela's Feast* and answering questions about your thoughts. Discuss your thoughts with your partner.

• On one side of an index card, write down any questions you had about the text. On the other side, write down the answer you and your partner discuss.

Long Vowels in Context

Reread *Abuela's Feast* to find words with long vowels. Then write three sentences about the transfer of heat. Be sure that each sentence includes at least two long-vowel words. Exchange your sentences with a partner and circle the words with long vowels.

Turn and Talk

ASK QUESTIONS

Discuss with a partner what you have learned so far about asking questions.

• What does it mean to ask questions while you read?

• Why should you ask questions about what you read?

Choose one of the questions you created about *Abuela's Feast*. Discuss with a partner why you asked the question and how you found the answer.

Critical Thinking

With a group, identify the three types of heat transfer. Using *Abuela's Feast*, write descriptions of the three types of heat transfer. Then discuss answers to these questions.

• Why do you think a fan is an important part of a convection oven?

• What does this story tell you about how convection, conduction, and radiation differ?

• Why do you think Abuela plans to use the microwave to heat the soup?

Ovens, Ovens, Ovens!

Baking a cake may be a **chemical** reaction, but you do not need to be **scientific** to choose which oven is best for you. Let us help you choose a new oven, or two!

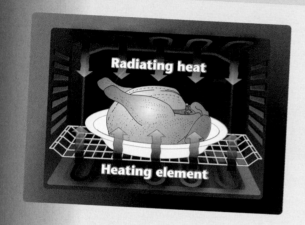

Conventional Ovens

Many cooks feel most comfortable using a conventional oven. This type of oven transfers heat through **conduction** and radiation. In the case of conduction, the heat moves from the source of the heat to the food through direct contact. The heat also radiates through the air to the food. This type of oven cooks food from the outside in.

Convection Ovens

Ovens that use **convection** are another popular choice. These ovens use a fan to move hot air inside the oven. This type of oven also cooks food from the outside in. However, since the hot air surrounds the food, food cooks faster and more evenly than in a standard oven.

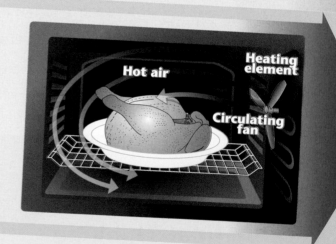

Microwave Ovens

Microwave ovens cook food in a completely different way. They heat only the **molecules** inside the food. The air inside the oven does not get hot, so food cooks from the inside out.

Energy is absorbed by food and converted into heat

Structured Vocabulary Discussion

With a partner, examine the vocabulary words above. Then, read the phrases below. For each, say the vocabulary word that comes to mind and explain the reason for your choice.

flow of heat through direct contact

flow of heat through moving air

Throughout the week, add to your vocabulary journal entries. Record new insights and other words that relate to this week's vocabulary.

Picture It

Copy this word organizer into your vocabulary journal. Fill in the boxes with things that are **scientific**.

scientific

The study of how heat is transferred is scientific.

Copy this word web into your vocabulary journal. Fill in the circles with examples of **chemical** reactions.

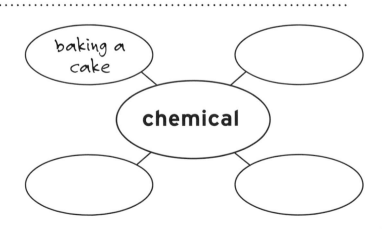

baking a cake

chemical

The Heat Is On!

Ever since the discovery of fire, people have looked for ways to use heat to cook food. Here are a few of the many solutions people have found.

MUD OVENS Native Americans in the Southwest used mud ovens to bake bread. People still use mud ovens today.

Traditional Native American mud ovens, called a beehive oven

Homesteader's mud oven

Clay oven being constructed in Afghanistan

MICROWAVE OVENS

The first microwave stood nearly 6 ft tall and weighed over 750 lbs. Electromagnetic waves in a microwave heat the molecules in food.

First commercial microwave, 1947

Modern microwave

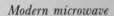

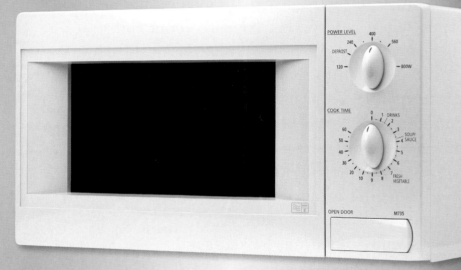

SOLAR OVEN The Sun's radiation energy reflects on the surface of the oven and transfers heat to the food.

Solar oven

TV Review

The SCIENTIFIC Gourmet!

Do you like cooking shows? If you do, here's a new one with a real twist—*The Scientific Gourmet*. Chef Tom Lang presents a wacky mix of cooking and chemistry in every show. This is the type of television that you can find only on a public-access station in the Midwest. It's long on humor and short on fancy gadgets. I'm not sure about ability.

Lang—all decked out like a mad scientist—doesn't believe it's enough to show you how to make a beautiful soufflé. He wants you to know how chemical reactions and heat make the thing rise.

On one episode, Lang made pancakes six different ways. After the third batch, I realized he was trying for a range of flavors, from very sweet to tart to just plain yucky. The ones with cranberries looked good. They bubbled nicely as he dropped the chunky batter on a very hot griddle. But the ones with lots of chili powder had to taste awful. After he choked down a bite, he said in hoarse whisper, "If you can't take the heat, get out of the kitchen." I think he should stick around for awhile—just for laughs.

Nouns

Activity One

About Nouns

A noun names a person, place, thing, or idea. Most common nouns—such as *children, kitchen,* and *science*—refer to general persons, places, things, or ideas. A proper noun refers to a specific person, place, or thing, such as *Emily* or *United States*. Proper nouns usually begin with a capital letter. As your teacher reads *The Scientific Gourmet*, listen for the nouns.

Nouns in Context

With a partner, read *The Scientific Gourmet*. Find as many nouns as you can and write them in the correct category in a chart like the one below.

PEOPLE OR ANIMALS	PLACES	THINGS	IDEAS
Tom Lang	Midwest	gadgets	humor

Activity Two

Explore Words Together

Look at the list of words on the right. Work with a partner to determine whether each noun is a person, place, thing, or idea. Then, together think of two additional nouns for each category.

student	altitude
First Avenue	comfort
bonfire	duty

Activity Three

Explore Words in Writing

Brainstorm a list of nouns that could fit in a description of a cooking show. Then, using your list, write two sentences to add to the review of *The Scientific Gourmet* cooking show.

Let's Get Cooking!

by Ruth Siburt

Every time I see a cake, I think of my mother, Lou Ann Siburt. She is always baking or cooking something. Cakes are her specialty. I conducted the following interview with my mother while home on a visit. I guess you never really stop learning from your parents!

Q **You are a professional cake decorator, baker, and mother of seven. I would guess you've done a lot of cooking in your life.**

A That's right. I suppose if you added it all up, you could say I'd been cooking and baking for well over sixty years. That would mean about 64,000 plus meals. At first, I cooked for my family at home. Later I worked for commercial bakeries in the community.

How do you think Lou Ann Siburt came up with the number of meals she has cooked?

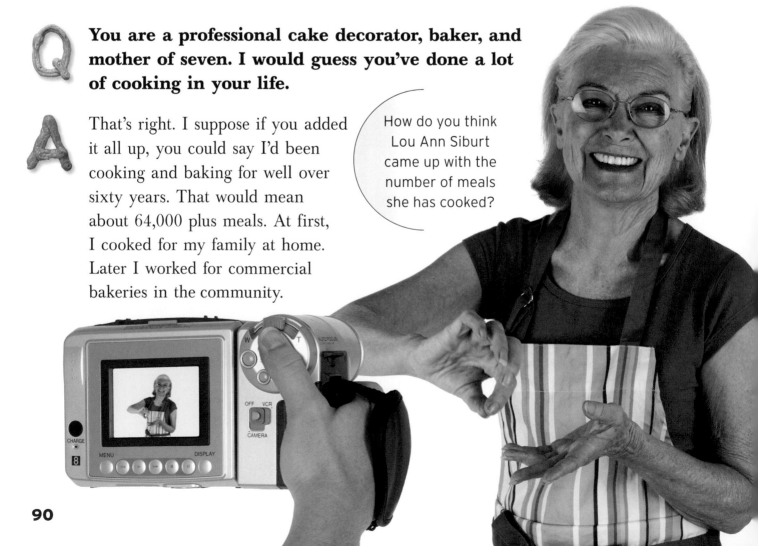

 Q **Do you ever think about the science behind all of the cooking you do?**

 A While I was preparing the meals for my family, I wasn't thinking about science. However, now I do know a good bit about the science behind cooking.

 Q **Can you explain some things to me about heat and the way it is transferred during cooking? What is conduction, for instance?**

 A Think about cooking pancakes on top of the stove in a pan. First, the pan gets hot from the burner's flame. Then the hot pan transfers its heat to the batter, which browns into nice pancakes. The metal pan acts as a "conductor" of heat. You have to flip the pancake to cook it on the other side. The heat comes from only one direction and travels through something solid (in this instance, the metal of the pan). That's conduction.

Cooking with conduction

Why would a cook need to understand the transfer of heat?

 Q **What other types of heat transfer are used regularly in cooking? What about microwaves? How do they transfer heat to cook food?**

 A Microwaves cook by a heating method known as radiation. Electromagnetic waves travel through the air. The waves don't need a solid, such as metal, to heat up the food. Also, the waves enter the food from more than one direction at a time. That speeds up the cooking process.

Dessert in a Bakery

 You used to work in a commercial bakery. Was that a much different experience than baking at home?

Say Something Technique Take turns reading a section of text, covering it up, and then saying something about it to your partner. You may say any thought or idea that the text brings to mind.

 Oh, yes. For one thing we were making things in much larger amounts. When I first started working in a commercial bakery we had a huge, conventional oven. We could bake up to eight cake layers at once. That's enough to build two three-tiered wedding cakes. We filled the pans with cake batter and placed them on one of the three racks, which rotated in the same sort of way a Ferris wheel rotates. That helped the layers bake evenly, but it was still the conduction-type of baking because the heat came from only one direction. The cake layers rotated through the heated air inside the oven. Later we upgraded to a convection-type of oven.

Do you think that cakes baked in a conventional oven at home bake evenly without rotating racks? Why or why not?

How was the convection oven different? Why did you consider it an upgrade?

We could still bake up to eight layers at once, but with the convection-type oven the layers were still. A fan in the back of the oven forced heated air around all sides of the layers. The heat came from above the layers and below and all around the sides. The convection ovens reduced the amount of baking time by quite a few minutes. Plus, we didn't have to turn the oven heat up as high as in the conventional oven. All of these factors meant we could bake more cakes in less time and use less energy. Convection really baked the cakes!

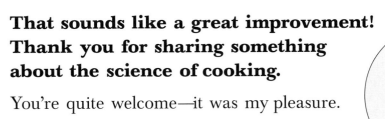 **That sounds like a great improvement! Thank you for sharing something about the science of cooking.**

Why are the improvements in oven technology so important?

You're quite welcome—it was my pleasure.

Comparing Ovens

Which type of oven or ovens would be best if you needed to cook for a large family? Why?	Conventional Oven	Convection Oven	Microwave Oven
Heat Source	Heat is generated by heat coils.	Heat is generated by heat coils.	Food is cooked by high-frequency electromagnetic waves. The waves generate heat by causing molecules within the food to vibrate.
Heat Transfer	Heat is transferred through direct contact. It also radiates from the hot surfaces, such as racks, to the food.	Fans constantly move hot air around the inside of the oven.	Heat is transferred within the food from the vibrating molecules.
Direction of Heat When Baking	Heat primarily cooks the food from below.	Heat cooks the food from above, below, and the sides.	Food cooks from the inside out.
Oven's Internal Temperature	The temperature within the oven is uneven. Also, items on the lower rack block some of the heat from reaching the upper racks.	The temperature within the oven is relatively even, since the hot air can move freely around the oven.	The food is cooked without warming the air around the food.
Cooking Times and Energy Use	Conventional ovens are the slowest of the three forms of ovens and cook at higher temperatures.	Convection ovens cook more quickly, at lower temperatures, and use about 20 percent less energy than conventional ovens.	Microwave ovens cook foods the fastest and can reduce energy costs by as much as two thirds, but they do not cook all foods well.

Think and Respond

Reflect and Write

- You and your partner have read *Let's Get Cooking!* and said something about your reading. Discuss your comments with your partner.

- On one side of an index card write an inference you made from the text. On the other side of the card, explain the details that helped you make the inference. Discuss your inferences with your partner.

Nouns in Context

Reread *Let's Get Cooking!* to find examples of nouns. Write down the words you find. Then use some of the nouns to create a short advertisement for a convection oven. Share your advertisement with a partner.

Turn and Talk

INFER

With a partner, discuss what you have learned about how to infer.

- What does it mean to infer, or make an inference?

- Why is making an inference an important reading skill?

Choose one inference you made while reading *Let's Get Cooking!* Explain that inference to your partner.

Critical Thinking

With a partner, discuss the three kinds of cooking methods: conduction, convection, and microwave. Return to *Let's Get Cooking!* Write down details about each type of cooking oven. Then discuss these questions.

- Which oven would a large bakery probably choose?

- Why can't a microwave be used to cook all types of food?

- Why is contact with a hot surface needed in an oven that uses conduction?

What Is Sound?

Contents

Modeled Reading

Shared Reading

Interactive Reading

DUKE ELLINGTON

Appreciative Listening

Appreciative listening is listening for particular words or phrases that you enjoy hearing. Listen to the focus questions your teacher will read to you.

by Andrea Davis Pinkney

illustrated by Brian Pinkney

Duke Ellington

by Ernestine Giesecke

"Da Duke" Ellington and "Sweet Pea" Billy Strayhorn,

A thumping stray horn, to announce a train.

A saxophone train, a *Black and Tan Fantasy* train,

Hear a **harmony** on the train, a muted trumpet train.

Now I can hear them **improvise** a train.

Oh what a train, not just a train, a fading 'A' train.

You gonna take it? Gonna find a stray horn?

Gonna *Take the 'A' Train?*

Now there's a beat, an umpy-dump beat.

A *Money Jungle* beat, umpy-dump, umpy-dump,

From Duke's jumpin' band, he **broadcast** to the world.

Hits you with a Club, a wicked Cotton Club.

All up under the clarinet, an exotic pounding beat.

And Bubber Miley's trumpet growls the **melody**.

A jolly *Tiger Rag*, a singing trombone.

And a wordless singer's *Creole Love Call.*

Growlin' band's umpy-dump brush sheds a *Blue Light,*

Wakes a *Blue Goose,* spreads *C Jam Blues.*

An **experiment** with color: "Can't Eat Here" blues.

Blue mood, *Jungle Blue* band, umpy-dump.

Structured Vocabulary Discussion

When you teacher says a vocabulary word, your small group will take turns saying the first word you think of. After a few seconds, your teacher will say, "Stop." The last person in your group who said a word should explain how that word is related to the vocabulary word your teacher started with.

Throughout the week, add to your vocabulary journal entries. Record new insights and other words that relate to this week's vocabulary.

Picture It

Copy this word web into your vocabulary journal. Fill in the circles with words that describe a **melody**.

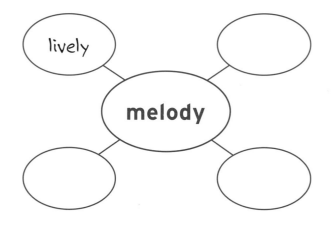

lively

melody

Copy this word wheel into your vocabulary journal. Fill in the sections with ways a musician might **experiment** while writing a song.

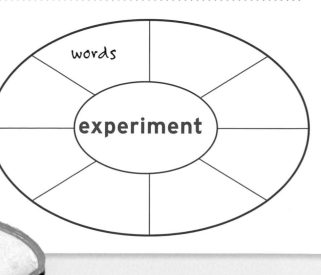

words

experiment

Comprehension Strategy

Determine Importance

Not all information in a selection is of equal importance. To understand what you read, learn to determine importance. As you read, identify the main ideas and supporting details. Then separate the important information from the information that is interesting but not important. These steps will help you decide what is and is not important in the text.

Think about the most **IMPORTANT** ideas.

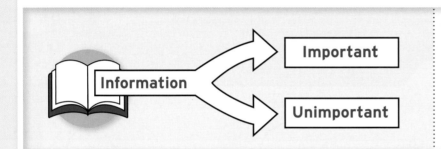

Think about information you notice as you read. Then decide if it is important or just interesting.

TURN AND TALK Listen as your teacher reads the following lines from *Duke Ellington*. With a partner, read the passage again. Look for the important information. Then discuss these questions.

• What is the main idea of the passage?

• What details does the author give to support the main idea?

• What information is interesting but not important?

The word on Duke and his band spread, from New York to Macon to Kalamazoo and on to the sunshiny Hollywood Hills. The whole country soon swung to Duke's beat. Once folks got a taste of Duke's soul-sweet music, they hurried to the record stores, asking:

"Yo, you got the Duke?

"Slide me some King of the Keys, please!"

"Gonna play me that Piano Prince and his band!"

People bought Duke's records—thousands of them.

TAKE IT WITH YOU Knowing what is important makes you a better reader. As you read other selections, try to determine importance. Use a chart like this one to help you as you read.

Information That I Noticed	Important?	Explain Your Thinking
"The whole country soon swung to Duke's beat."	☑ **Important** ☐ **Unimportant but Interesting**	This information tells how popular Duke was. That's the main idea.
"Slide me some King of the Keys, please."	☐ **Important** ☑ **Unimportant but Interesting**	The way people talked is interesting, but it's not particularly important.

Genre
Poem

Riding the Sound Waves

by Ruth Siburt

Uncle Rafe was my exhibit for the Science Fair

His musical vibrations moved much more than air.

Jazz and Blues or Rock and Pop

When he gets a place pumpin', it never stops.

Rafe ripped a riff so wild and true

It lifted my Mrs. Masters clear out of her shoes

Whirled her 'round the gym and then

Set her back in her shoes again.

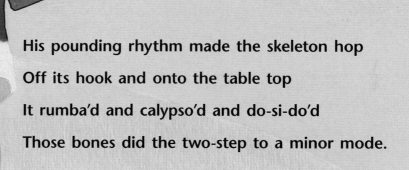

His pounding rhythm made the skeleton hop
Off its hook and onto the table top
It rumba'd and calypso'd and do-si-do'd
Those bones did the two-step to a minor mode.

At straight up noon, Uncle Rafe swung low.
And his cool vibrations made ketchup lava flow
Across the floor and loop d' loop
It sailed right through the basketball hoop.

Uncle's music moved us all in a major way.
Yeah, my ribbon was blue at the end of the day!
You should've heard those science judges rave,
When we showed them how to ride a sound wave.

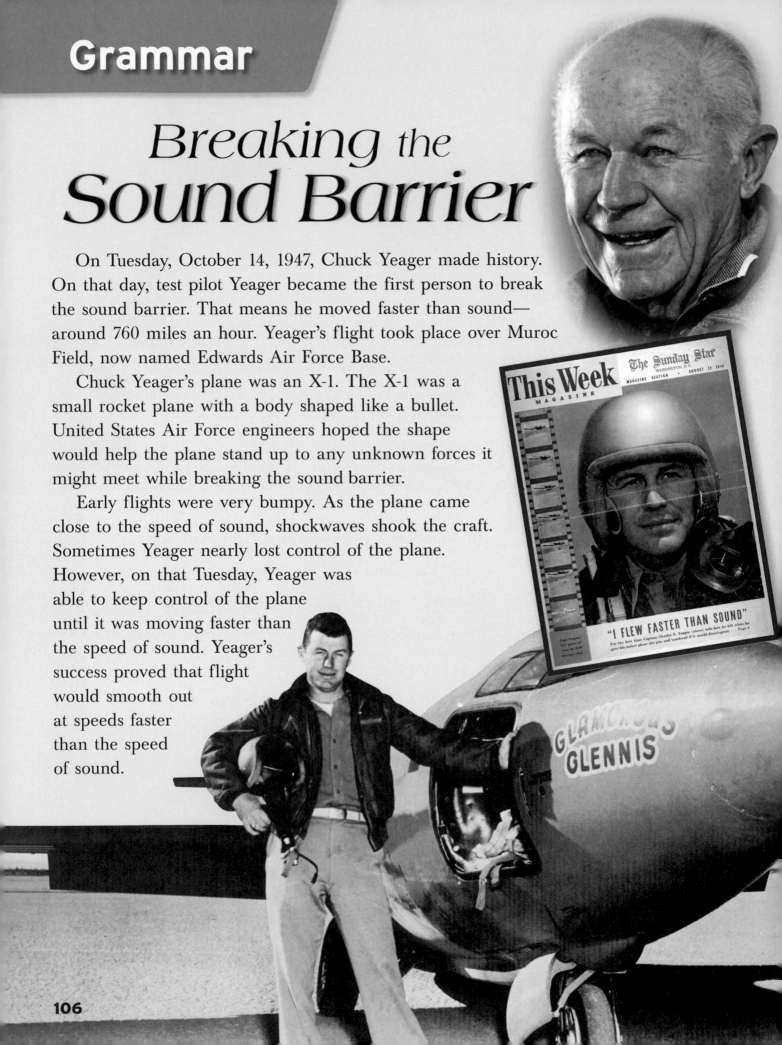

Breaking the Sound Barrier

On Tuesday, October 14, 1947, Chuck Yeager made history. On that day, test pilot Yeager became the first person to break the sound barrier. That means he moved faster than sound— around 760 miles an hour. Yeager's flight took place over Muroc Field, now named Edwards Air Force Base.

Chuck Yeager's plane was an X-1. The X-1 was a small rocket plane with a body shaped like a bullet. United States Air Force engineers hoped the shape would help the plane stand up to any unknown forces it might meet while breaking the sound barrier.

Early flights were very bumpy. As the plane came close to the speed of sound, shockwaves shook the craft. Sometimes Yeager nearly lost control of the plane. However, on that Tuesday, Yeager was able to keep control of the plane until it was moving faster than the speed of sound. Yeager's success proved that flight would smooth out at speeds faster than the speed of sound.

The Sunday Star

This Week
MAGAZINE

"I FLEW FASTER THAN SOUND"

GLAMOROUS GLENNIS

Proper Nouns

Activity One

About Proper Nouns

A proper noun names a specific person, place, or thing. Each important word in a proper noun begins with a capital letter. Your name is a proper noun; so is the country's name—the United States of America. As your teacher reads *Breaking the Sound Barrier*, listen for the proper nouns.

Proper Nouns in Context

With a partner, read *Breaking the Sound Barrier*. Find all of the nouns in a paragraph. Write the nouns in a chart like the one below. Then, indicate which ones are proper nouns, and why.

ALL NOUNS	IS IT A PROPER NOUN?	WHY?
Chuck Yeager	✓	person's name

Activity Two

Explore Words Together

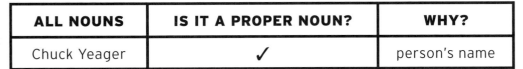

planet   sports team

teacher   newspaper

writer   song

With a partner, look at the list of words on the right. Make a list that contains examples of at least one proper noun for each noun in the list. Share your list with the class.

Activity Three

Explore Words in Writing

Find a magazine, newspaper, or book you like. Choose an interesting paragraph that contains proper nouns. Write the paragraph on a sheet of paper. Circle the proper nouns. Think of other proper nouns that could fit in the sentences instead of the ones in the original paragraph. Rewrite the paragraph using your choice of proper nouns. Share your paragraph with a partner.

Sounds Good to Me!

by Mary Dylewski

Sound is everywhere. Birds chirp sweetly on a warm, spring day. A musician plays a gentle melody on a flute. Thunder booms during a downpour. But, what is *sound*? Most dictionaries define *sound* as anything that can be heard. Scientists define *sound* as energy that travels in vibrating waves. We hear sound when these vibrating waves make an object or the material around it move. I spent a few hours touring sound exhibits at the science museum to find out more.

1:00 p.m. Exhibit 1—Speak Up, Please

This exhibit explores what laughing, crying, singing, and shouting have in common. People make these sounds using folds of tissue called vocal cords. As air passes between these folds, the folds vibrate to produce sounds. Children's vocal cords are short, and they cause the air to vibrate very quickly. This produces sounds with a high pitch. In adults, the vibration of air is much slower, producing sounds with a lower pitch.

What is the important information in this log entry?

1:15 p.m. Exhibit 2—I Can Hear You

    This exhibit shows how the ear works. The outer part of a person's ear collects sound waves as the waves travel through the air. These waves strike tiny bones in the middle ear and cause them to vibrate. The inner ear picks up the vibrations, and the brain recognizes them as sound. People who have difficulty hearing may benefit from a hearing aid. A hearing aid is a device that makes sounds louder.

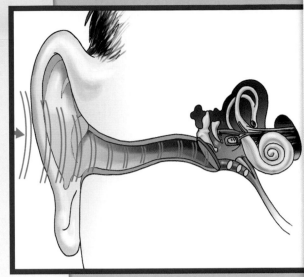

Sound	Decibels
Silence	0 dB
Quiet whisper	10 dB
Rustling leaves	20 dB
Loud whisper	30 dB
Average home	40 dB
Normal conversation	60 dB
Busy street	70 dB
Vacuum cleaner	80 dB
Portable music player at maximum level	100 dB
Chain saw	117 dB
Jet plane	130 dB

1:30 p.m. Exhibit 3—Now Hear This!

    This exhibit compares the loudness of different sounds. Scientists measure loudness in decibels (dB). A busy street is louder than an average home. Sounds louder than a vacuum cleaner can cause hearing loss over time. Very loud sounds, like jet planes, can cause immediate hearing loss.

    This chart shows a few sounds that the exhibit compared.

Would you describe the chart as important or interesting but unimportant? Explain your answer.

Say Something Technique Take turns reading a section of text, covering it up, and then saying something about it to your partner. You may say any thought or idea that the text brings to your mind.

1:50 p.m. Exhibit 4—Echoes . . . echoes . . . echoes

This exhibit demonstrates how animals use echoes. An echo occurs when sound waves bounce back to the object that made the sounds. Some animals use echoes for survival. Bats, for example, use echoes to navigate around dark caves. As they fly, they make high pitched sounds. By sensing the time it takes for the sound waves to return, bats avoid bumping into the cave's walls. Bats also use these echoes to find food.

What helps you find important information on this page?

2:05 p.m. Exhibit 5—Mapping the Sea

This exhibit shows how scientists use sonar to map the ocean floor. *Sonar* is short for "SOund NAvigation and Ranging." Sonar devices take advantage of the fact that sound travels well through water. Scientists produce a beeping sound at the surface. They then wait to see how long it takes the sound wave to hit a solid object and bounce back to the surface as an echo. The closer the object, the less time it will take for the sound waves to come back. Sound waves that bounce off underwater mountain peaks take less time to return than sound waves that bounce off the deep ocean floor.

2:05 p.m. Exhibit 6—The Sounds of Music

This exhibit explains how musical instruments produce sound. Guitars and other stringed instruments produce sound when musicians strum or bow the strings. The length, thickness, and tension of the strings determine pitch—how high or low the sound is. Long, thick, loose strings vibrate slowly to produce a low pitch. Short, thin, tight strings vibrate quickly to produce a high pitch. Musicians put their fingers in different places on the neck of guitars or violins to change the sound.

How does the title of this section give you a clue to what is important in the text?

Flutes and other wind instruments produce sounds when musicians force air into them. The pitch depends on the amount of air in the instrument. Large amounts of air vibrate slowly and produce a low pitch. Smaller amounts of air vibrate quickly and produce a high pitch. Musicians control the amount of air by opening and closing holes on the instruments.

Some drums and other percussion instruments produce sound when musicians strike them. Others produce sounds when musicians shake them. Shaking causes the air pressure around the instruments to change. We hear the changes in air pressure as sound.

2:35 p.m. Exhibit 7—Thunder

This exhibit looks at thunder. Thunder is the sound that follows lightning. When lightning heats up the air nearby, the air pressure suddenly rises and produces a wave. As this wave travels through the air, it causes the rumbling sound we call thunder. I liked the exhibit's instructions on how to use lightning and thunder to estimate my distance from a storm.

1. Count the number of seconds between when you see the lightning and hear the thunder.

Why might it be important to know how close a storm is?

2. Divide the number of seconds by 5.

3. The product is your approximate distance from the storm in miles!

2:45 p.m. Exhibit 8—The Telephone

I learned from this exhibit how telephones send sound. I use phones every day. But I never thought about how they work. The answer is electricity! A phone changes a person's voice into electric signals. The phone then sends the signals over telephone lines or through the air to another phone. That phone changes the signals back into sound.

Think and Respond

Reflect and Write

- You and your partner took turns reading aloud sections of *Sounds Good to Me!* Discuss the thoughts or ideas you had as you read.

- Choose one of the sections you read, and write down the details you found on index cards. On the other side of each index card, explain why that detail was important or interesting but unimportant.

Proper Nouns in Context

Reread *Sounds Good to Me!* to find examples of proper nouns. Write down the words you find. Then look for common nouns in the observation log. Provide examples of proper nouns for each of the common nouns on your list. For example, *Atlantic Ocean* is a proper noun for the common noun *ocean*. Share your lists with a partner.

Turn and Talk

DETERMINE IMPORTANCE

Discuss with a partner what you have learned so far about determining importance.

- How do you determine importance?

- How does determining importance help you understand what you read?

Choose one important piece of information from *Sounds Good to Me!* Discuss what made that information important rather than interesting but unimportant.

Critical Thinking

With a group, discuss what you know about sounds and vibrations. Write in the center of a piece of paper "Sounds are Vibrations." Around that statement, write down the names of all the exhibits in *Sounds Good to Me!* Then discuss the following questions together.

- Why are vibrations important in the production of sound?

- Why are echoes important to bats, to scientists mapping the sea bottom, and to musicians?

- Why is it important that sound can be changed into electric signals?

Making Music

A violin is a stringed **instrument** for making music. Violin strings vibrate when a musician plucks them or draws a bow across them. A string's **vibration**, or back and forth motion, creates sound.

To make music, a violin must be correctly tuned. Musicians **concentrate** on each string's sound as they turn a tuning key to tighten or loosen the string. Small changes in how tight the strings are change the way they vibrate. Certain vibrations create a musical tone, or **pitch**. When all four strings vibrate properly, the violin is ready to make music.

Changing the **length** of the strings also changes the way they vibrate. As they play, musicians use their fingers to press the strings against the fingerboard. This shortens the vibrating part of the string and creates different musical tones.

Structured Vocabulary Discussion

Work with a partner or in a small group to fill in the following blanks. Be sure you can explain how the words are related.

Attempt is to *try* as *focus* is to _____.

_____ is to *violin* as *animal* is to *giraffe*.

Throughout the week, add to your vocabulary journal entries. Record new insights and other words that relate to this week's vocabulary.

Picture It

Copy this word web into your vocabulary journal. Fill in the circles with things that have a **length**.

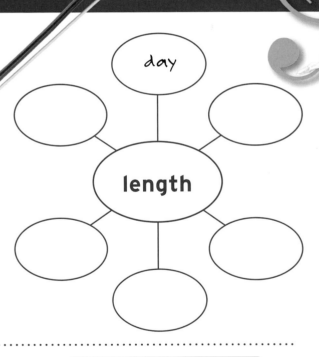

day

length

Copy this word organizer into your vocabulary journal. Fill in the boxes with words that could be used to describe a **pitch**.

pitch

shrill

I LOVE A PIANO

by Irving Berlin

As a child I went wild when a band played.

How I ran to the man when his hand swayed.

Clarinets were my pets, and a slide trombone I thought was simply divine

But today, when they play, I could miss them.

Ev'ry bar is a jar to my system.

But there's one musical instrument that I call mine . . .

[chorus:]

I love a piano, I love a piano.

I love to hear somebody play

Upon a piano, a grand piano.

It simply carries me away.

116

I know a fine way to tickle a piano my way.
I love to run my fingers o'er the keys, the ivories.

And with the pedal I love to meddle,
When the composer comes this way.
I'm so delighted, if I'm invited
To hear that long haired genius play.

So you can keep your fiddle and your bow.
Give me a P-I-A-N-O, oh, oh!
I love to stop right beside an upright
Or a high toned Baby Grand!

WHERE DO WE Find THAT?

Instant Message ▬ ▢ ✕

Conversation   Edit   View   Contact   Help

Grneyes: Our assignment is to write a report on the history of the recording industry. I found this definition online.

Record industry

The **record industry** is the part of the <u>music industry</u> that earns <u>profit</u> by selling <u>sound</u> <u>recordings</u> of <u>music</u>.

I don't suppose we can do all our research on the Internet, do you think?

LilSis: I don't think so. I'll start researching recording technology. I'll use the encyclopedia in the library. I'll also start gathering background information about important inventors. I think we should put a time line in the report.

Grneyes: Great idea! Be sure to list the books, almanacs, and other references you use. We'll get extra points if we include a bibliography.

LilSis: Will do. How about a graph about money in the industry? Maybe we should show how much is spent on recordings each year or which artist earned the most. I should be able to find that in an almanac.

Grneyes: Sounds good. Can you drop a dictionary at my locker? My younger brother took mine.

LilSis: No problem, I'll drop it off before math class. Will we need to find populations or geographical information from an atlas?

Grneyes: Don't think so. Got to run.

Send |

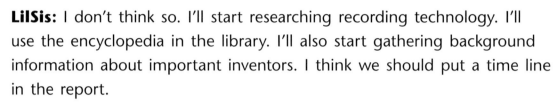

Reference Materials

Activity One

About Reference Materials

Reference materials are sources that provide information. Encyclopedias provide information about many topics. Atlases show where places are located. Dictionaries tell the meanings of words as well as the pronunciation, part of speech, and origin of the words. Almanacs usually come out each year and give facts about many subjects. Listen for these words as your teacher reads the message exchange between Grneyes and LilSis.

Reference Materials in Context

With a partner, read *Where Do We Find That?* Find the names of the reference materials in the passage and write them in the correct category in the chart.

INFORMATION ABOUT LOCATIONS	INFORMATION ABOUT WORDS	INFORMATION ABOUT TOPICS
		encyclopedia

Activity Two

Explore Words Together

Look at the list of words on the right. Work with a partner to determine what type of information you are most likely to find in each source. Create a list for each type of reference material. Share your list with the class.

almanac   encyclopedia

atlas   Internet

dictionary   bibliography

Activity Three

Explore Words in Writing

Choose one of the types of reference materials from the list. Use that source to research something about the recording industry. Then use your research to write a paragraph. Share your paragraph with a partner.

The Smell of Soup and the Sound of Money—

A Tale from Turkey   retold by Melissa Blackwell Burke

Long ago, there lived a man who had fallen on hard times. He became a traveler, wandering from place to place, begging for money to buy food. Many people ignored him, causing the man great despair. One day, a woman spotted the traveler through a thick crowd, and she took pity on him. Without saying a word, she held out her hand and offered the man a piece of bread. The woman had little to give, and this was all she could spare.

The woman's generosity startled the traveler. Nobody had paid attention to him like this before. When he tried to thank the woman, she turned abruptly and hurried on her way. As she disappeared into the crowd, the man began to smile. For the first time in weeks, he felt hope. He looked at his piece of bread in amazement and thought, "How nice it would be if I had something to put on this bread!"

What questions about the story does the title cause you to ask?

120

The traveler quickly walked to the nearest inn. He approached the innkeeper and asked for some food to eat with his bread. The innkeeper was not fond of beggars, and waved him away in disgust. As the traveler turned to leave, he noticed a delicious smell drifting from the kitchen. He peeked in, and saw a large pot of soup bubbling over a fire.

"This soup smells wonderful," thought the traveler. "If only there were a way to get a taste." The traveler was becoming discouraged, but he then had a brilliant idea. He could hold his piece of bread over the steam. Surely this would capture some of the soup's taste. The traveler walked toward the pot, until it was within arm's length. He then extended his arm above the pot, holding the bread carefully between his fingers.

"Thief!" an angry voice shouted from the doorway. The startled traveler spun around in shock. The innkeeper dashed wildly into the kitchen and violently seized the traveler's arm. "Thief!" the innkeeper cried again. "You have stolen my soup!"

What questions could you ask about the innkeeper's reaction to the traveler?

Reverse Think-Aloud Technique Listen as your partner reads part of the text aloud. Choose a point in the text to stop your partner and ask what he or she is thinking about the text at that moment. Then switch roles with your partner.

The traveler was astonished. "But innkeeper," he pleaded, "I assure you I have stolen nothing. I was simply enjoying the smell of the soup." The innkeeper glared at the traveler and replied, "You are a thief, and I will prove that you are guilty of stealing."

The innkeeper dragged the traveler to a desk near the front of the inn. He opened a dictionary and said, "Read the definition of *steal* for me."

What question could you ask that would require a dictionary to answer?

The traveler read, "To *steal* is to take something that does not belong to you without permission or without paying."

The innkeeper looked at the traveler and said, "You took something that did not belong to you. You did not have permission, and you did not pay. You are guilty of stealing."

The traveler tried to explain, "I already told you that I did not take any soup." The innkeeper pointed his finger at the man and replied, "Ah, but you admit that you took the smell. You must pay for the smell!"

The traveler was very surprised by this. He explained that he had no money. The innkeeper became very angry. He insisted that the traveler go before a judge.

As they walked to the judge, the innkeeper thought about how the judge might settle this. Perhaps the traveler would be forced to work at the inn. The traveler also thought about what the judge might do, and he felt miserable at the thought.

A wise man named Hodja was serving as the judge at that time. When the two arrived, he listened patiently as the innkeeper made his complaint. Hodja then allowed the traveler to explain his side of the story. When both were finished talking, Hodja was silent. He took time to concentrate on the matter before him. As the innkeeper and the traveler watched, Hodja studied a thick encyclopedia of law.

What kind of questions do you think an encyclopedia of law answers?

Finally, Hodja addressed the innkeeper. "You demand payment for the smell of your soup," he said. "Is that correct?" The innkeeper shook his head eagerly in reply, "Yes, I do." Hodja then addressed the traveler. "But you have no money to pay. Is that correct?" The traveler looked sadly toward the floor and answered, "That is correct."

Hodja looked toward both men and said, "I believe I have a fitting solution." With that, he took two shiny coins from his pocket. He asked the innkeeper to step forward, and the innkeeper smiled. Hodja held the coins next to the innkeeper's ear and banged them together. The coins made an unmistakable clanging noise. "And now you have your payment," said Hodja.

The innkeeper was puzzled, and he asked, "What do you mean?" Hodja looked directly at the innkeeper and replied, "The traveler did not eat your soup, and yet you demand payment. Did you not just hear the sound of money? It seems to me that the sound of money is fair payment for the smell of soup."

What kinds of things do you wonder about on this page?

The innkeeper was dumbfounded, and the traveler started to grin. With that, the judge stood up and said, "Now, innkeeper, go back to your inn. Traveler, continue on your journey!"

Think and Respond

Reflect and Write

- You and your partner took turns reading and sharing your thoughts about *The Smell of Soup and the Sound of Money*. Discuss the questions you had and the answers you found to them.

- Choose three questions, and write them on index cards. On the other side of each index card, write the answers you found to your questions.

Reference Materials in Context

Reread *The Smell of Soup and the Sound of Money* to find examples of words related to reference materials. Then, write a short paragraph answering the following question: "How do the characters in the folktale use reference materials to support their arguments?" Share your paragraph with a partner.

Turn and Talk

ASK QUESTIONS

Discuss with a partner what you have learned so far about how to ask questions.

- What does it mean to ask questions when you read?

- When and why should you ask questions about what you read?

Choose one of the questions you asked about *The Smell of Soup and the Sound of Money*. Discuss with a partner why you asked the question and how you found the answer.

Critical Thinking

With a group, discuss the characters in *The Smell of Soup and The Sound of Money*. Create a three-column chart on a piece of paper. Title the columns "traveler," "innkeeper," and "judge." Brainstorm a list of words that describe how each person felt about the events in the story. Then discuss these questions together.

- Was a crime committed in the story? Explain.

- What was each character's response to the accusation of a crime?

- Do you think justice was served in the story? Why or why not?

How Goes the War on Poverty? 1965
Norman Rockwell (1894–1978)

Proud to Be an
AMERICAN

Viewing

The artist who painted this picture was Norman Rockwell. He painted pictures of ordinary people doing ordinary things. This painting shows his reaction to the War on Poverty that President Lyndon Johnson declared in the 1960s. A poster of this painting has these words from President Johnson added: "Hope for the Poor; Achievement for Yourself; Greatness for your Nation."

1. How would you describe the people in the painting? Why do you think the painting shows only the faces and eyes of some people and not of others?

2. Who or what do you think the hands and their placement in the painting represent?

3. How does the quotation from President Lyndon Johnson add meaning to the painting? What do the words mean?

In This UNIT

In this unit, you will read stories about the U.S. Constitution, the Bill of Rights, and the national government. You will also read about how people like Harriet Tubman have worked to protect the rights of others.

THEME 5

Let Freedom Ring

Contents

Modeled Reading

Shared Reading

Interactive Reading

PAPA'S MARK

by
GWENDOLYN BATTLE-LAVERT

illustrated by
COLIN BOOTMAN

Precise Listening

Precise listening means listening for details. Listen to the focus questions your teacher will read to you.

Whom Should I Believe?

Concord, January 31, 1788

Dear Thomas,

Thank you for your letter of January 15. You are right about the **Constitution**. There is quite a **battle** raging between the Federalists and Anti-Federalists. I, too, have been following the debate. But I must admit I still don't know which side I favor.

Many of my friends here in Massachusetts are more clear than I am. They are worried about the Constitution. They think it will give too much power to the federal government. Like the Anti-Federalists, they would like power to stay with the states. Most are **tracing** their argument to our state's long history of town meetings. My friends think that we have already proven that we can govern well.

Still, I have to agree with the Federalists. The current Congress has too little power. We need a central government that can raise money. We also need one that can help with trade. I watch the local merchants **huddled** together discussing what will happen if the Constitution fails. As for me, I think I want a Bill of Rights. But surely the process of making an **amendment** will make that possible.

Your friend,

George

Structured Vocabulary Discussion

When your teacher says a vocabulary word, have the people in your group take turns saying the first word they think of. Continue until your teacher says, "Stop." Then have the last person who said a word explain how his or her word is related to the vocabulary word.

Throughout the week, add to your vocabulary journal entries. Record new insights and other words that relate to this week's vocabulary.

Picture It

Copy this word organizer into your vocabulary journal. Fill in the ovals with words that mean the same as **amendment**, and list examples of documents that could have an amendment.

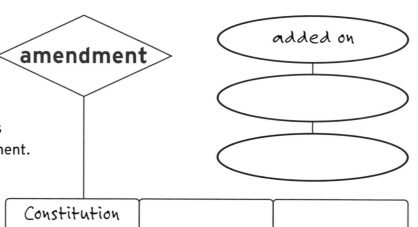

Copy this word wheel into your vocabulary journal. In the upper sections, give synonyms for **tracing** used as a noun. In the bottom section, give synonyms for tracing used as a verb.

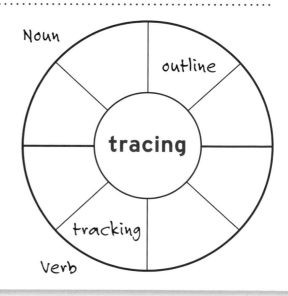

Monitor Understanding

As you read, take time to monitor your understanding. Every so often, stop and make sure you understand what you have read thus far. If you realize you do not understand something, take action. For example, reread, use reading strategies, or ask yourself questions.

Check to make sure you are **UNDERSTANDING** what you read.

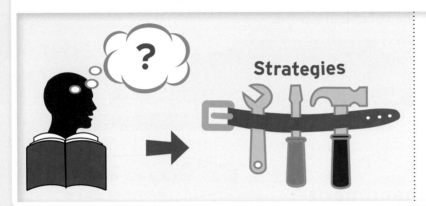

Strategies

Check your understanding. When you don't understand, try a few key strategies to help.

TURN AND TALK Listen to your teacher read the following passage from *Papa's Mark*. Then with a partner, reread the lines and describe what has happened by answering the following questions.

• What does Mr. Jones decide to do with Samuel T.?

• How does Papa vote?

• Why does Papa want Simms to help him put the ballot in the box?

Out of the crowd came Mr. Jones, the storekeeper. "Samuel T.," he said, "I'm voting with you."
The two men walked together across the town square into the courthouse.
"I'm Samuel T. Blow," said Papa. "I've come to vote."
"Make your mark," said the clerk.
Simms said, "My Papa can sign his name."
Papa wrote his name. The clerk handed him a ballot. Papa made a choice.
Then he said, "Simms, come over here. Let's put the ballot in the box together."
Simms grinned. Papa voted. Lamar County changed.

TAKE IT WITH YOU Describing what you have read is a good way to monitor understanding. If you cannot describe what has already happened, then use strategies that will help you. As you read other selections, use a chart like the one below to help you monitor understanding.

Page Where I Noticed I Didn't Understand	What I Did						Which One Worked?
	Reread	Reflected On Purpose	Thought About Meaning	Asked Myself Questions	Thought About Strategies	Used Genre Knowledge	
I didn't understand why Mr. Jones wanted to vote with Samuel T.	✔	✔	✔	✔	✔	✔	I asked myself who Mr. Jones was. When I reread, I remembered that Mr. Jones likes Samuel T. When I thought about meaning, I understood that the county changed because the two men could now vote together.

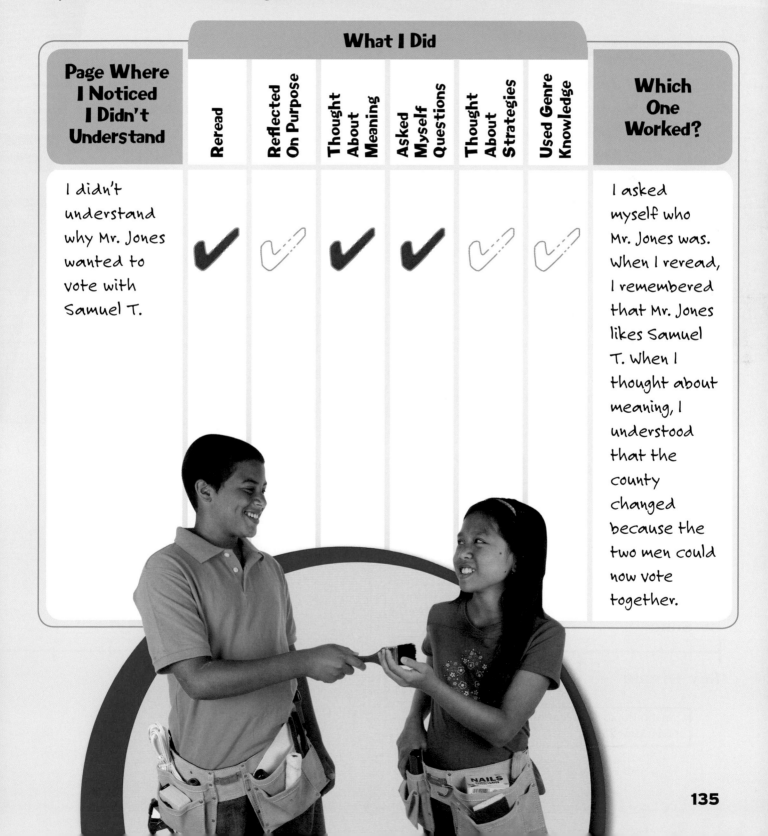

James Madison
Father of the Constitution

by Sue Miller

James Madison was born in Virginia in 1751. His parents owned a plantation near the Blue Ridge Mountains. Young James loved books and learning. At 18, he left home for college in New Jersey. There he learned new ideas about government. Madison left college firmly believing that good government and freedom go hand in hand. He was also sure that a good government requires a balance of power. These views would play important roles in the future of the United States.

After college, James Madison entered politics. During the Revolutionary War, the states had banded together under the Articles of Confederation. Under the Articles, Congress could do little more than make war and enter into treaties. The states held all the power. But the states often worked against each other. Some people feared the country would fall apart.

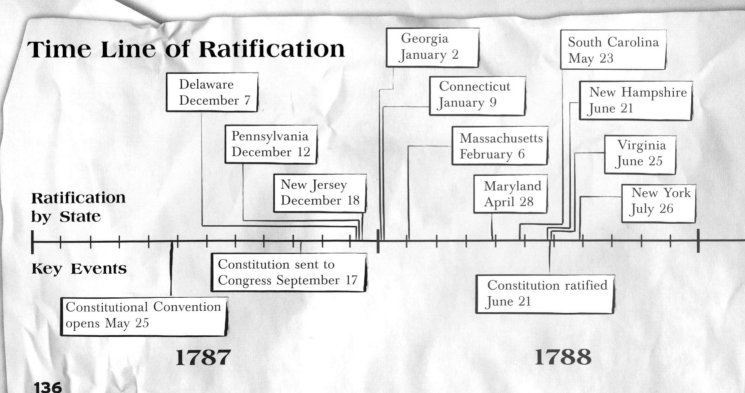

Time Line of Ratification

Georgia
January 2

South Carolina
May 23

Delaware
December 7

Connecticut
January 9

New Hampshire
June 21

Pennsylvania
December 12

Massachusetts
February 6

Virginia
June 25

New Jersey
December 18

Maryland
April 28

New York
July 26

**Ratification
by State**

Key Events

Constitution sent to
Congress September 17

Constitution ratified
June 21

Constitutional Convention
opens May 25

1787

1788

Madison was a Federalist. Federalists thought the states had too much power. Federalists wanted a strong national government. They believed such a government could protect the country and help it grow. They convinced Congress to call a convention to "fix" the Articles. But the Federalists' goal was to write a new constitution.

The convention began in May 1787. Madison set forth a new plan. The government would have three branches—executive, legislative, and judicial. Each branch would balance the power of the other branches. This arrangement would protect people's freedoms. The Anti-Federalists protested. They wanted to keep power in the hands of the states. They also wanted a Bill of Rights. The convention battle was difficult. Gaining state approval was even harder. The Federalists finally won after they promised to add a Bill of Rights. One of Madison's first acts as a member of the new government was to draft the Bill of Rights— the first ten amendments to the U.S. Constitution.

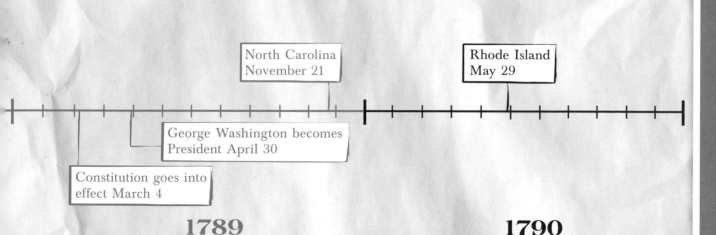

North Carolina
November 21

Rhode Island
May 29

George Washington becomes
President April 30

Constitution goes into
effect March 4

1789   1790

THE CONSTITUTION OF THE UNITED STATES

Did You Know? Some people disagreed with the idea of a strong central government. The Constitution might not have been approved if its backers had not promised a Bill of Rights. It was agreed that these amendments would be added as soon as possible. The Bill of Rights consists of the first ten amendments to the Constitution. It grants certain rights to the people. The First Amendment, for instance, gives people the right to free speech.

Better Late Than Never

George Washington arrived a day early for the Constitutional Convention in 1787. But the meeting was delayed for 11 days. Many of the delegates arrived late. Once the meeting started, people were hired to guard the doors. They were there to protect the privacy of the meeting.

Say Yes

The framers of the Constitution could not count their work as an achievement until a total of nine states approved the document. Without nine states, the framers' efforts would have been a failure. The framers also wanted "Yes" votes from New York and Virginia, since these were two important states.

Synonyms and Antonyms

Activity One

About Synonyms and Antonyms

A synonym is a word that has almost the same meaning as another word. For example, *construct* is a synonym for *build*. An antonym is a word that means the opposite of another word. *Cheap* and *expensive* are antonyms. If a word has more than one synonym or antonym, pick the word that is closest to your intended meaning. As your teacher reads *The Constitution of the United States*, listen for synonyms and antonyms.

Synonyms and Antonyms in Context

With a partner, read *The Constitution of the United States* to find examples of synonyms and antonyms. Enter the words in a chart like the one below. For each word, supply the synonym, or antonym, or both.

WORD	SYNONYM	ANTONYM
delayed	late	early

Activity Two

Explore Words Together

Look at the list of the words on the right. Take turns with a partner supplying a synonym or an antonym for each word.

freedom	debt
birth	dull
loss	continue

Activity Three

Explore Words in Writing

Choose three of the words you used in the last activity. Write a sentence that uses the synonym you chose for that word. Then write a sentence that uses the antonym for that word. Share your sentences with a partner.

A Not Very WELL-KEPT SECRET

by John Manos

I was 11 years old when the Constitutional Convention drafted the U.S. Constitution. I worked at an inn that was close to the Pennsylvania State House. That is the building in which the Declaration of Independence was signed! My job was to wait on the men who wrote the Constitution. My father told me the Constitution was important. He pointed at the flag we fly outside our house. It has 13 stripes on the flag. He said the Constitution would be the thread that held those stripes together.

I did not work by myself with all of the great men. Many other boys worked as waiters and helped around the inn. All summer we took care of delegates' rooms. As time passed, we began to identify with one man or another. For example, George Mason from Virginia was in one of my rooms. My friend Tom served Alexander Hamilton, from New York. Amos took care of James Madison. We all wanted Henry's job. He took care of George Washington! After a while we each started calling each other by the names of the delegates we helped.

How could you be sure you know what *wait on* means in the context of this passage?

Now, everyone knows that the Constitution was written in secret. The delegates met in locked rooms, and guards stood outside the shut doors to make sure that only certain people entered. But it wasn't much of a secret to us! While we brought the delegates food and made up their beds, all secrets were open to us! We heard every argument they had in the inn, and if truth be told, we heard a lot of arguing!

Of course, we each thought of the man whose room we tended as "our" delegate. And we took everything we heard that person say to heart. If I overheard George Mason say the Constitution was flawed, I agreed with him. If he said each person's rights should be spelled out, I was ready to fight for that idea. Tom said the federal government should be strong. Why? Because that is what Mr. Hamilton thought. We argued over all the articles of the Constitution.

What can you tell about the views of George Mason and Alexander Hamilton from this paragraph?

So one day, when "Hamilton" (Tom) said the central government should control everything, I guess I reacted badly. I picked up my piece of bread and threw it at Tom. It bounced off his forehead.

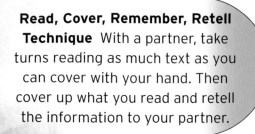

Read, Cover, Remember, Retell Technique With a partner, take turns reading as much text as you can cover with your hand. Then cover up what you read and retell the information to your partner.

There was a little pause. It was like the calm moment after a lightning bolt, a preamble to the thunder that is sure to follow. Boy, did it follow. Tom practically flew off his bench, and unhappily for me, he had his bowl of vegetables in his hand. While I was trying to shake peas out of my eyes, "Randolph"—the boy who looked after Edmund Randolph from Virginia—heaved a tomato across the room. It missed "Hamilton," but it smacked "Washington" (Henry) in the back of the head. This was bad—Henry hated tomatoes; he thought they were poison. I'm not sure if George Washington would have agreed. But in this case, Henry didn't care.

What could you do if you had trouble understanding this page? Explain.

Henry put a hand to his hair, and then he screamed when he saw tomato seeds between his fingers. When I say, "screamed," I don't mean some little shout, I mean a glass-breaking shriek, a sound that would stab you in the ears. I think he's still embarrassed about it. After that loud, scary scream, everyone in the room stood still for a second or two.

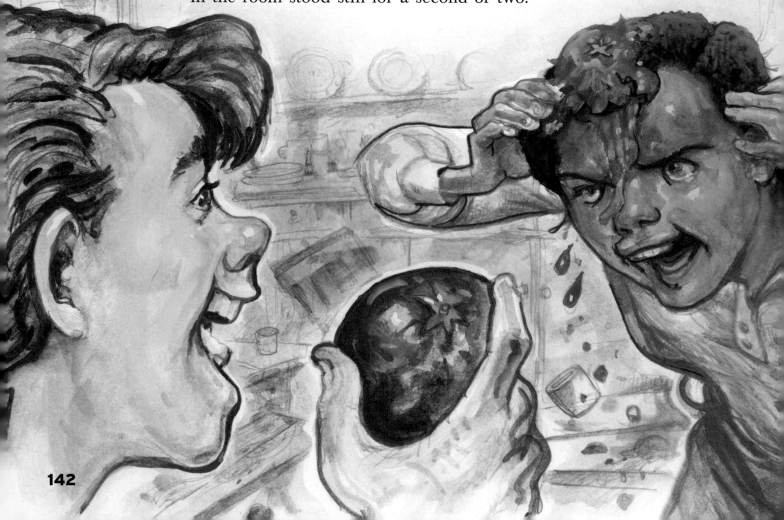

Then Henry picked up a huge melon and threw it at "Madison" (Amos). Luckily, "Madison" was quicker than he looked and was able to duck. But after that, the room was out of control. Food flew everywhere. I was covered in fruit and stew—not a single article of my clothing was clean; even my shoes had crushed carrots in them. Seeing that Tom was looking my way, I yelled, "The states need their rights protected," and then ducked as parsnips flew by my ear.

At that moment Benjamin Franklin—yes, *the* Ben Franklin—hobbled into the dining room (his gout was obviously bothering him a great deal). We all wanted to melt into the floor. Mr. Franklin looked around, surveying the scene. He picked up an apple and took a bite out of it, and then used the apple to point around the room. "Who got this started?" he asked. I finally stepped forward. He stared at me as if he was angry, but his eyes were twinkling—at least I hope they were. "You had better clean up this mess," he said, as he turned to leave. "Something extremely important is about to happen."

What might you do if you do not know what event Ben Franklin is talking about?

I was down on my knees scrubbing the floor. Tom, Amos, and Henry were scooping up smashed food. We were all silently trying to figure out what to say to our parents once the inn's owner returned and found what we had done—no one was going to be happy.

Suddenly, the doors flew open. "They've signed it!" a man shouted. "They have a Constitution to present to Congress! The delegates are leaving the building." Everyone cheered. It was September 17, 1787, a date I'll never forget.

Only 41 of the 55 delegates were still in Philadelphia, and only 39 of them signed. One delegate was sick, but he added his vote. Of course, it took until 1788 for enough states to approve the Constitution so it could take effect. My man, George Mason, would not sign. He said it needed a Bill of Rights. Two other men refused to sign for the same reason. But just last year, in 1791, ten amendments were added. People are calling those first ten amendments the "Bill of Rights." I hope George Mason is pleased.

What strategies could you use if you had trouble understanding this page?

Think and Respond

Reflect and Write

- You and your partner took turns reading parts of *A Not Very Well-Kept Secret*. Discuss the information you retold to each other.

- Choose two parts of the story that were hard to understand. On one side of an index card, write down the problem. On the other side, write down what action you took to understand the problem information.

Synonyms and Antonyms in Context

Reread *A Not Very Well-Kept Secret* to find examples of synonyms and antonyms. Then work with a partner to write a short diary entry describing the food fight. Include in the entry synonyms and antonyms for at least four words. Share your diary entry with the class.

Turn and Talk

MONITOR UNDERSTANDING

Discuss with a partner what you have learned so far about how to monitor understanding.

- What does it mean to monitor understanding?

- What can you do when you don't understand something you've read?

Review the unclear details you described for *A Not Very Well-Kept Secret*. Then, with your partner, determine which strategy you can use to try to understand the problem information.

Critical Thinking

With a group, talk about the ways that authors use symbols. Discuss the food fight in *A Not Very Well-Kept Secret*. Return to the text and write down the name of each boy and the names of the delegate with whom each boy identified. Discuss these questions together.

- Why do you think the boys identified with the framers of the Constitution?

- Why do you think the boys got into a food fight?

- What does the food fight represent?

RATIFY NOW!

GeorgeWashington

John Adams

Thomas Jefferson

James Madison

Inform yourself with the facts. The **Articles** of Confederation—the set of rules that govern us—are beyond repair. The United States needs a strong central government that can raise money, raise an army, and work to pay off our war debts. We need to expand trade and secure our borders. These are not tasks that the states can carry out on their own.

The delegates to the convention took care to **draft** a document that will stand the test of time. The new Constitution sets up three branches of government: executive, legislative, and judicial.

The power of each branch is checked by the other branches. Power will not be in the hands of the few. The rights of individuals will be protected. Does not the **preamble** state "We the People"?

For those still worried, a **Bill** of Rights has been promised. It will be added in due time. This Bill of Rights will protect basic rights. Among these will be freedom of religion, freedom of speech, freedom of the press, and the right to gather peacefully.

Structured Vocabulary Discussion

Work with a partner to complete the following sentences about your vocabulary words.

What might a person *draft*, a letter or a salad? Explain your answer.

What might you use to *inform* someone of important news, a personal letter or a grocery list? Explain your answer.

Throughout the week, add to your vocabulary journal entries. Record new insights and other words that relate to this week's vocabulary.

Picture It

Copy this word organizer into your vocabulary journal. Fill in the boxes with synonyms for the word **preamble**.

> **preamble**
>
> opening
>
> [ ]
>
> [ ]

Copy this word web into your vocabulary journal. Research the different meanings of the word **bill**. Then fill in the circles with things that mean the same thing as bill.

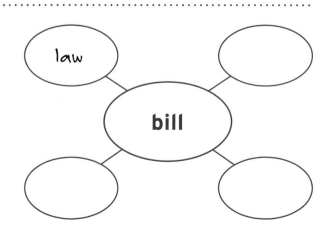

The Bill of Rights

by Abby Jones

I'm a part of *we the people*,
A *we* that's made of individuals,
Individuals who can take shelter
Under certain basic rights
Just to read a paper
Or watch the evening news

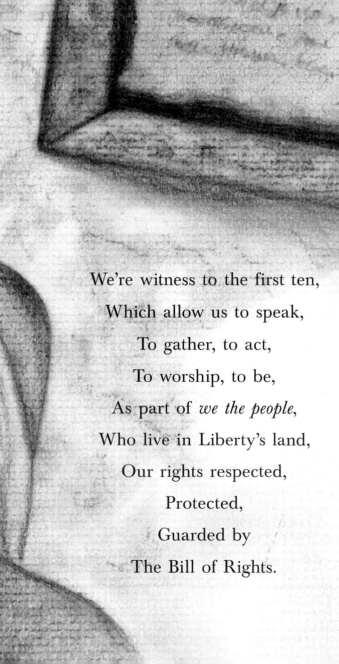

We're witness to the first ten,
Which allow us to speak,
To gather, to act,
To worship, to be,
As part of *we the people*,
Who live in Liberty's land,
Our rights respected,
Protected,
Guarded by
The Bill of Rights.

These Rights are RIGHT for US

NOTES

The First Amendment states five basic freedoms.

Freedom of Religion: Congress cannot establish an official religion. People get to choose their own religions. Later, the Supreme Court ruled that states also have to follow this law.

Freedom of Speech: People have the right to state their views, even if others do not think the views are right.

Freedom of the Press: The government cannot press its views on the press.

Freedom of Assembly: People have the right to gather in one place in order to place their views on record.

Freedom of Petition: People have the right to complain to a government official about unfair treatment.

Cesar Chavez

It's #1

Many people think the First Amendment is the most important amendment in the Bill of Rights. Why? In this respect: It protects the freedoms that form the basis of democratic government. The First Amendment guarantees that the government will respect the rights of all people.

Multiple-Meaning Words

Activity One

About Multiple-Meaning Words

A multiple-meaning word has more than one meaning with the same spelling. For example, *address* can mean the place you live. It can also mean to say something to someone. As you teacher reads *These Rights are RIGHT for US*, listen for multiple-meaning words.

Multiple-Meaning Words in Context

With a partner, read *These Rights are RIGHT for US*. Write down each multiple-meaning word that you find in a chart like the one below. Then list two meanings for the word.

WORD	FIRST MEANING	SECOND MEANING
state	To say	One part in the U.S.

Activity Two

Explore Words Together

With a partner, look at the list of words on the right. Discuss what different meanings the words can have. Then take turns creating sentences using the correct meanings.

object	subject
compact	bound
record	racket

Activity Three

Explore Words in Writing

Write a short paragraph telling three things you have learned about the U.S. Constitution. In your paragraph, be sure to use at least three multiple-meaning words in two different ways each. Exchange your paragraph with a partner and see if your partner can locate and define the words.

Harriet Tubman
LEADS THE WAY

by Kathleen Krull

When Harriet Tubman was seven years old, she took a lump of sugar from the kitchen table when she thought no one was looking. She knew her mistress would object. But Harriet never got sweets, and the object looked so inviting. Unfortunately, the mistress caught Harriet as she reached her fingers inside the bowl. Harriet knew she would be punished, so she ran quickly from the house. She continued to run until she found a pigpen in which to hide. For four days, the terrified young girl hid among the pigs, eating their scraps. Finally, starving, Harriet went back to the house. There was no place safe to hide, no place to go, and no way out of slavery.

What information do you think is most important in this paragraph?

Harriet Tubman was born a slave on the Eastern Shore, near Bucktown, Maryland. Slave life was cruel and uncertain. Slaves worked hard for no money. They could be sold at any time, and families were often torn apart. Harriet's parents–Harriet Green and Benjamin Ross–were luckier than some couples. Even though they worked for different masters, they were often able to live near each other.

Harriet Tubman

Slaves could not go to school, so Harriet was put to work at age five cleaning house and babysitting. Harriet would have preferred to work outside with her father. She liked to help him plow the fields, plant and harvest crops, and chop wood. Benjamin Ross taught his daughter how to use the stars as a compass and how to tell if a wild plant was safe to eat. Harriet grew strong, but there still seemed no way out of slavery. Escape was dangerous business—many slaves chose not to try, and for those that did try, success was far from certain. When a slave escaped, the flight was publicized, and men with guns and dogs hunted the runaways.

Why might the skills Harriet Tubman learned from her father be important information?

But something secret was going on. It was called the Underground Railroad. The Underground Railroad wasn't under the ground. And it wasn't a railroad. It was a network of people who helped escaped slaves make their way to freedom in the North. The network included "conductors" and "station masters." Conductors acted as guides. Station masters provided safe houses. Both risked their own safety to help others escape from slavery. The dangers were particularly great for free African Americans. They risked being sent into slavery.

LAKE ONTARIO

Two-Word Technique
Write down two words that reflect your thoughts about each page. Discuss them with your partner.

When Harriet Tubman was 29, she heard that she was about to be sold. She gathered all her courage and decided to run away, even though it meant leaving her family behind. She packed her favorite quilt, some cornbread, and some fish. Harriet walked through the woods to find a woman who helped runaways. Shaky with fear, she knocked on the woman's door. The woman took her inside and told her what to do. Harriet was to follow the Choptank River north until it ended; she was then to cross into Delaware at Camden. The woman told Harriet to look for a white farmhouse with green shutters. There, someone would inform her about how to get to Pennsylvania and freedom. Harriet was so thankful that she gave the woman her quilt.

What information on this page is interesting but not important?

Harriet walked all night, hiding during the day. Finally, she found the white house with green shutters. That night, the family put Harriet in their wagon, covered her with vegetables, and took her to the next safe house. From there, Harriet headed north along the coast.

Traveling on the Underground Railroad

PENNSYLVANIA

MARYLAND

Baltimore

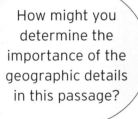

How might you determine the importance of the geographic details in this passage?

To the east was the Atlantic Ocean, to the west was the Chesapeake Bay, and in between were swamps. Harriet walked for 90 long miles. One grand morning, she finally arrived in the city of Philadelphia, Pennsylvania. "I felt like I was in heaven," Harriet said later. "I looked at my hands to see if I was the same person now that I was free."

From Pennsylvania, Harriet went on to New Jersey. She then settled in Auburn, New York. A year after her escape, Harriet heard bad news. Her favorite niece Kizzy and Kizzy's two children were about to be separated and sold. Harriet made the dangerous trip back into the South. She led Kizzy and her children to freedom. On her second trip, she rescued a brother. Later she was able to rescue her parents and much of her family. Harriet began leading strangers, too. In all, Harriet made at least 15 of those dangerous trips, conducting hundreds of slaves to freedom. "I never lost a passenger," she said proudly.

"I looked at my hands to see if I was the same person: now I was free. There was such a glory over everything. I felt like I was in heaven."

HARRIET TUBMAN

The Civil War ended the Underground Railroad. But Harriet's work was not done. During the war, she helped African Americans in the South. She also was a nurse to injured or unwell soldiers.

The war did something else. It helped bring an end to slavery. On January 31, 1865, Congress finally was able to draft the Thirteenth Amendment, which banned slavery. Congress then sent the amendment to the states for approval. It became law on December 18, 1865. Harriet was surely pleased.

How do the details of the Thirteenth Amendment fit with the rest of the article? Explain your answer.

In 1868, African American leader Frederick Douglass sent the following letter to Harriet Tubman.

August 29, 1868

The difference between us is very marked. Most that I have done and suffered in the service of our cause has been in public, and I have received much encouragement at every step of the way. You, on the other hand, have labored in a private way. I have wrought in the day—you in the night. I have had the applause of the crowd and the satisfaction that comes of being approved by the multitude, while the most that you have done has been witnessed by a few trembling, scarred, and foot-sore bondmen and women, whom you have led out of the house of bondage, and whose heartfelt "God bless you" has been your only reward.

Harriet Tubman

Think and Respond

Reflect and Write

• You and your partner have read *Harriet Tubman Leads the Way*. Discuss the thoughts that each of you shared.

• Choose two of the thoughts you shared. On one side of an index card, write the thought. On the other side of the index card write whether the thought related to an important or an unimportant detail.

Multiple-Meaning Words in Context

Reread *Harriet Tubman Leads the Way* to find examples of multiple-meaning words. Write down the words you find. Then write a short note from the perspective of a safe-house owner thanking Harriet Tubman for her work. Use at least four multiple-meaning words in the note. Share your note with a partner.

Turn and Talk Review

DETERMINE IMPORTANCE

Discuss with a partner what you have learned so far about how to determine importance.

• How do you determine importance?

• How does determining importance help you understand what you read?

Select four details from *Harriet Tubman Leads the Way*. Explain to a partner why each detail is important or unimportant.

Critical Thinking

With a group, brainstorm a list of words or phrases that describe the Underground Railroad and write them down. Return to *Harriet Tubman Leads the Way* and write how Harriet Tubman escaped from slavery. Discuss answers to these questions together.

• How was the Underground Railroad organized?

• Why do you think Harriet Tubman was willing to risk her own freedom and safety to help other people?

Contents

How the U.S. Government Works

by Syl Sobel

The Executive Branch

The Legislative Branch

The Judicial Branch

Strategic Listening

Strategic listening means listening to synthesize information in the selection. Listen to the focus questions your teacher will read to you.

Executive Branch

Legislative Branch

Judicial Branch

The Branches of Government

The Three Branches The U.S. government has three branches. The Constitution outlines the duties of each branch. It also establishes ways for each branch to balance the power of the other branches. The framers of the Constitution believed that this balance would protect **democracy**.

Article I of the Constitution outlines the duties of the **legislative** branch. This branch includes the two houses of **Congress**—the Senate and the House of Representatives. The main duty of this branch is to make laws.

Article II of the Constitution outlines the duties of the executive branch. The president is the head of this branch. The executive branch also includes the vice president and members of the cabinet. One of the duties of this branch is to **enforce** the laws made by Congress.

Article III of the Constitution outlines the duties of the judicial branch, which includes the Supreme Court and other federal courts. This branch decides what the laws mean. The president has the power to **appoint** judges, but Congress must approve each choice.

Structured Vocabulary Discussion

Work with a partner or in a small group to fill in the following blanks. Be sure you can explain how the words are related.

California is to *United States* as *Senate* is to _____.

Divide is to *separate* as _____ is to *uphold rules*.

Throughout the week, add to your vocabulary journal entries. Record new insights and other words that relate to this week's vocabulary.

Picture It

Copy this word organizer into your vocabulary journal. Fill in the ovals with words that explain what it means to **appoint**. List in the boxes examples of people who can appoint others.

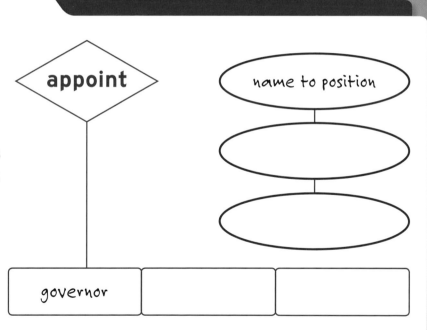

appoint

name to position

governor

Copy this word organizer into your vocabulary journal. Fill in the boxes with things people can **enforce**.

enforce

The police can enforce laws.

Synthesize

As you read, take time to synthesize information. Synthesizing involves more than simply summarizing the big ideas in what you are reading. When you synthesize, you combine ideas to create new ideas that increase your understanding.

To **SYNTHESIZE** means to use existing ideas to come up with a new idea.

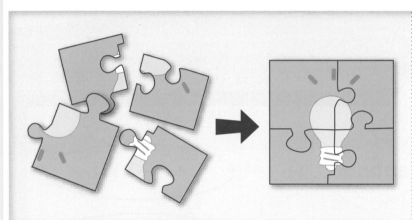

Think about what you have read and find the important ideas. Then use these ideas to create a new idea.

TURN AND TALK Listen to your teacher read the following lines from *How the U.S. Government Works*. Then with a partner, read the lines and see if you can use the information to create a new idea. Discuss the following questions with your partner.

• What are the ideas in the passage?

• What new idea about taxes can you create from these ideas?

Some of the most important laws that Congress makes are about money. The government spends money to do its jobs. The government gets the money it needs from the people who live in the United States. The money that people pay to the government is called *taxes*. Congress decides how much taxes the government can collect from the people. These taxes pay for the work of the U.S. government. Congress also makes laws that say when people have to pay taxes to the government and how much to pay.

TAKE IT WITH YOU To synthesize, first determine the important ideas in what you are reading. Then you use these ideas to create new ideas. As you read other selections, use a chart like the one below to help synthesize information.

After Reading I Know That...

Congress makes important laws about money.

The government spends money to do its jobs.

The government gets the money it needs from the people who live in the United States. The money that people pay to the government is called taxes.

Congress also makes laws that say when people have to pay taxes to the government and how much to pay.

This Information Helps Me Understand That...

The government can create new tax laws when it needs to raise more money for spending.

AN IMPORTANT Debate

by David Dreier

CAST OF CHARACTERS

John Stevens, Speaker of the House

Martha Green, Democratic Congresswoman from Oregon

Simon Rock, Republican Congressman from Idaho

Assorted other members of the House of Representatives, unnamed

Setting: A number of seats in rows facing a podium, stage left. The members of the House are in their seats chatting. Speaker Stevens, on the podium, pounds his gavel.

SPEAKER STEVENS: Let's come to order. We have some important business before us. We're considering a proposed bill to tear down the four dams on the Lower Snake River. For the opposition, I call on the Honorable Simon Rock of Idaho. Will you please sum up the arguments against this bill?

CONGRESSMAN ROCK: Thank you, Mister Speaker. There are two good reasons for keeping the dams. They generate electricity, and they have made it possible for freight barges to travel all the way to Lewiston, Idaho. Barge traffic has greatly boosted the economy of Lewiston, making it a seaport. Then, too, the dams have not harmed the salmon in the river in any major way. It makes no sense to remove the dams.

(*He takes his seat.*)

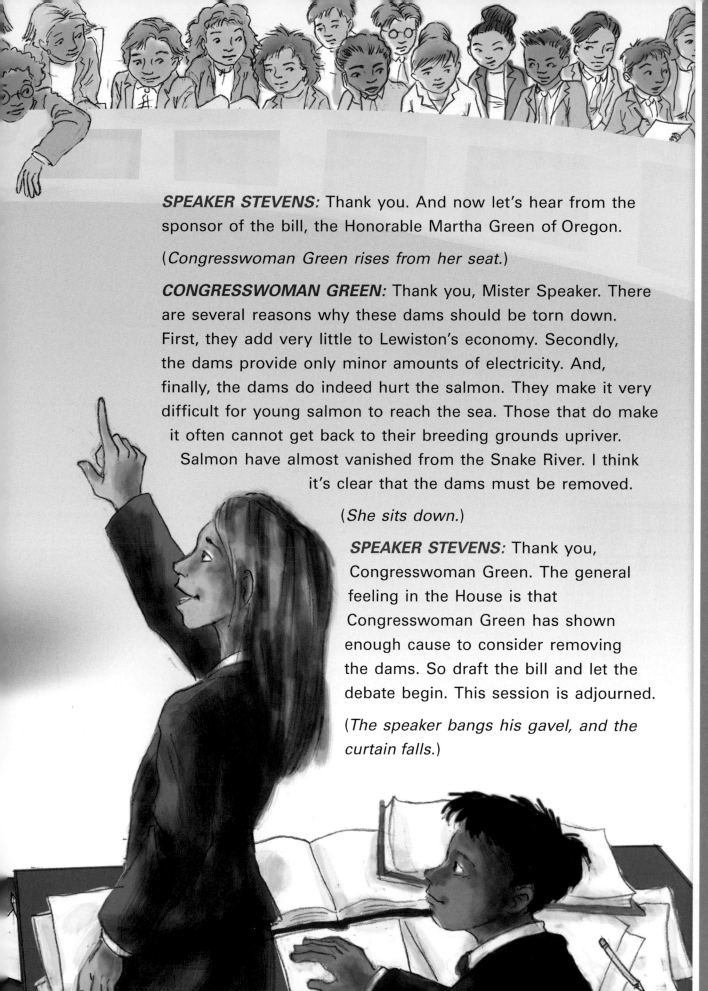

SPEAKER STEVENS: Thank you. And now let's hear from the sponsor of the bill, the Honorable Martha Green of Oregon.

(*Congresswoman Green rises from her seat.*)

CONGRESSWOMAN GREEN: Thank you, Mister Speaker. There are several reasons why these dams should be torn down. First, they add very little to Lewiston's economy. Secondly, the dams provide only minor amounts of electricity. And, finally, the dams do indeed hurt the salmon. They make it very difficult for young salmon to reach the sea. Those that do make it often cannot get back to their breeding grounds upriver. Salmon have almost vanished from the Snake River. I think it's clear that the dams must be removed.

(*She sits down.*)

SPEAKER STEVENS: Thank you, Congresswoman Green. The general feeling in the House is that Congresswoman Green has shown enough cause to consider removing the dams. So draft the bill and let the debate begin. This session is adjourned.

(*The speaker bangs his gavel, and the curtain falls.*)

Visting the Capital

Dear Mom and Dad,

Washington, D.C., is great, but my feet are killing me. We've walked all over the nation's capital for four days. Our teachers don't want us to waste an hour. I heard someone say we looked like a herd of Holstein cows in our black and white school uniforms. I thought it was funny, but it irritated Andy. He was already grumpy because he accidentally dropped money down a grate.

I really liked the U.S. Capitol Building. I already knew it was home to the House and Senate. But I learned that construction of the building started in 1793. Over the years, the government has added new sections. It now covers four acres!

We also went to the White House today—the president wasn't home. Did you know that the White House has 132 rooms, 35 bathrooms, 412 doors, 417 windows, and 28 fireplaces! It takes 570 gallons of paint to cover the outside. No way would I want to paint that house!

Well, I'd better close. I need to hang up my clothes and get ready for tomorrow—we're going to the Supreme Court.

Love,
Ben

Homonyms

Activity One

About Homonyms

Homonyms are words that sound the same but have different meanings and spellings. *Coarse* and *course* are examples of homonyms. When you hear such words, you can tell which word is meant by how it is used in the sentence. As your teacher reads *Visiting the Capital*, listen for the homonyms.

Homonyms in Context

With a small group, read *Visiting the Capital* to find homonyms. Write each pair of words and their meanings in a chart like the one below.

WORD	MEANING	HOMONYM	MEANING
for	In favor of	four	the number 4

Activity Two

Explore Words Together

The list on the right contains words that have homonyms. List the homonym for each word and define it. Then compare your list with a partner's.

tax	fair
bail	threw
berth	strait

Activity Three

Explore Words in Writing

Choose four homonym pairs from your Activity Two list. Write a short paragraph on any topic about government using your homonyms. Put each pair of homonyms as close together in the paragraph as you can. Share your paragraph with a partner.

Jefferson Memorial

Being a Judge

AN INTERVIEW WITH JULIA PACKARD

by John Manos

*A*rticle III of the Constitution established the Supreme Court. It also gave Congress the power to establish other types of courts. Congress set up U.S. District Courts and U.S. Courts of Appeals. It also set up a variety of special courts. These special courts hear specific types of cases. Tax courts are one example of a special court.

Federal judges deal with three areas of the law. One area is crime. A judge may have to decide if a person is guilty of a crime, such as theft. The second area is civil cases, or lawsuits. Lawsuits include almost every argument between people in which a crime has not happened. The third group involves people or companies with bad debts. These people or companies owe more money than they can repay right now. The judges help them plan a way to handle their bad debts.

From the information on this page, what new idea do you have about the powers of Congress?

Julia Packard is a federal judge. She has been a judge since 1980. Judge Packard took time out from her busy schedule to share details about her job.

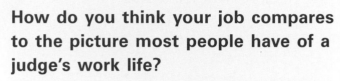

How do you think your job compares to the picture most people have of a judge's work life?

Most people think of the judges they see on television. Television judges all wear black robes and hear criminal cases. I'm not that kind of judge. I don't send people to jail. I'm an administrative law judge. I settle arguments between the federal government and people who work for the government.

Do you hear all your cases in one court, or do you need to travel to hear cases?

My office is here in Chicago, but I hear cases in an area of about 10 states. There are some 80 to 100 judges in my group. We all travel to hear cases. Yesterday I was in Milwaukee, Wisconsin. Next week I may be in Kansas City, Missouri. I am what is called a circuit judge. Abraham Lincoln rode a horse to hear cases in different towns in Illinois. This was called 'riding a circuit.' That is how we circuit judges got our name.

New Federal Cases in 2005

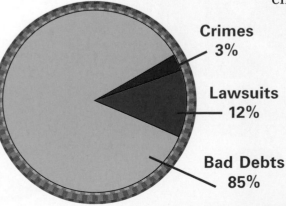

Crimes
3%

Lawsuits
12%

Bad Debts
85%

How would you describe Judge Packard's job based on the details here?

Read, Cover, Remember, Retell Technique
With a partner, take turns reading as much
text as you can cover with your hand.
Then cover up what you read and retell the
information to your partner.

What qualifications do you need to be a federal judge?

To become a federal judge, you must first be a lawyer.
So the first thing you have to do if you want to be a federal
judge is go to law school. Then you must be interested in
settling arguments between people—that is the
main part of the job. You want to make the
two sides happy in a case, but that isn't always
possible. You must be able to decide which
person has the law on his or her side.

What idea can you
synthesize from this
description of the
qualifications for becoming
a federal judge?

Some judges are elected; others are appointed. How did you get your job?

I am a federal judge—no federal judge is elected.
First, I had to meet certain qualifications. Then, I
had to apply for the position as a judge. No one had
to nominate me, like a Supreme Court judge. I was
appoinited to my position as a federal judge.

A judge presides in a court room.

172

What role do you play in the legal system?

I have the same role as all other judges. The legislative branch writes laws, and the executive branch sees that the laws are carried out. The judicial branch decides what the laws mean and how they should be carried out. Judges play a very important role in our country—they solve disputes so we don't have to fight over the laws.

What is your work as a federal judge like?

I may have ten cases per month, and I hear cases only three or four days of the month. All the rest of my time is spent either on the telephone talking to people involved in a case or writing decisions. If we can settle things over the telephone, people may not have to come to court. Once I have made a decision, I have to write it out in detail. So the biggest part of each month is spent writing.

How would you describe the judicial branch of the federal government, based on the details about Judge Packard?

What do you think is the most important part of your job as a federal judge?

I have learned that the most important part of my job is listening. A big part of being a judge has nothing to do with who is right and who is wrong. It simply involves listening. Even the people who are wrong want to be heard. They want to feel that they are not lost in the herd of other people who have problems. This is true in all kinds of situations that judges face. People want to know that someone will listen to them. Many people want to appear before a judge even when they know what they did was wrong. People want to explain *why* they did what they did. Once I have listened to their stories, I explain the law to them. When I explain to people why what they did was wrong, they usually agree with the decision, even though it goes against them. If people feel they have been heard, they trust the system. That is a wonderful thing about justice in the United States. Everyone can be heard.

Why do you think Judge Packard believes that the most important part of her job is listening?

EQUAL·JUSTICE·UNDER·LAW·

Think and Respond

Reflect and Write

• You and your partner took turns retelling sections of *Being a Judge*. Discuss your retelling.

• Choose two sections that you discussed. On an index card, identify an idea you synthesized from each section. On the back of the card, list the details that led to your synthesis.

Homonyms in Context

Reread *Being a Judge* to find examples of homonyms. Then work with a partner to use the word pairs in three sentences about the duties of a judge. Share your favorite sentence with the class.

Turn and Talk

SYNTHESIZE

Discuss with a partner what you have learned so far about how to synthesize information.

• What does it mean to synthesize?

• How can you put together ideas in what you read to create new ideas?

Review the details you listed for *Being a Judge*. Then, with your partner, use the details to create a new idea about what it means to be a judge.

Critical Thinking

With a group, identify the three big areas of law that federal judges handle. Write them down on the left side of a piece of paper. Return to *Being a Judge*. On the right side of the piece of paper, write down Julia Packard's duties as a judge. Discuss these questions together.

• Why do you think federal judges specialize in different areas of the law?

• How do you think Judge Packard's duties as a judge are similar to and different from the duties of other types of judges?

• What do you think is the most important part of being a judge?

MORE Than Just Delivering Mail

Dear Diary

I can't believe I'm finally in Washington, D.C., and actually working in the House of Representatives as a page. If I live to be 100, I'll never forget how thrilled I was when one of the House members from my state agreed to **nominate** me for consideration. It's a dream come true. I've wanted to be a House or Senate page since I was a little girl. I'm finally 16 and old enough. I know this is going to be my favorite memory from high school! How many kids get to spend a semester at the House Page School? I feel very lucky.

My government teacher says that one of the most important things we do as citizens is **elect** our government leaders. That's why she thinks this is such a great opportunity. I'll get to see how the House and Senate work with the **executive** and **judicial** branches. Government in action! She thinks that after it's all over, I'll **conclude** that the system is amazing. Me, too!

Tonya

Structured Vocabulary Discussion

Work with a partner to review all of your vocabulary words. Then choose the word that best matches these phrases. Discuss your choices with your partner.

before running for office   *like one who is in charge*

tying up loose ends   *like settling arguments*

> Throughout the week, add to your vocabulary journal entries. Record new insights and other words that relate to this week's vocabulary.

Picture It

Copy this word web into your vocabulary journal. Fill in the circles with people you can **elect**.

President

elect

Copy this word organizer into your vocabulary journal. Fill in the boxes with the responsibilities of the **judicial** branch of government.

interpret the Constitution

judicial

A THREE-PART MASTERPIECE

by Ruth Siburt

"We the People of the United States of America . . . ."

1600 Pennsylvania Avenue—the White House
Its East and West Wings cradling a strong center
Mirroring the three branches of government
Home to America's presidents who
Enforce her laws, design her policies, command her armies—
1600 Pennsylvania Avenue
Seat of power

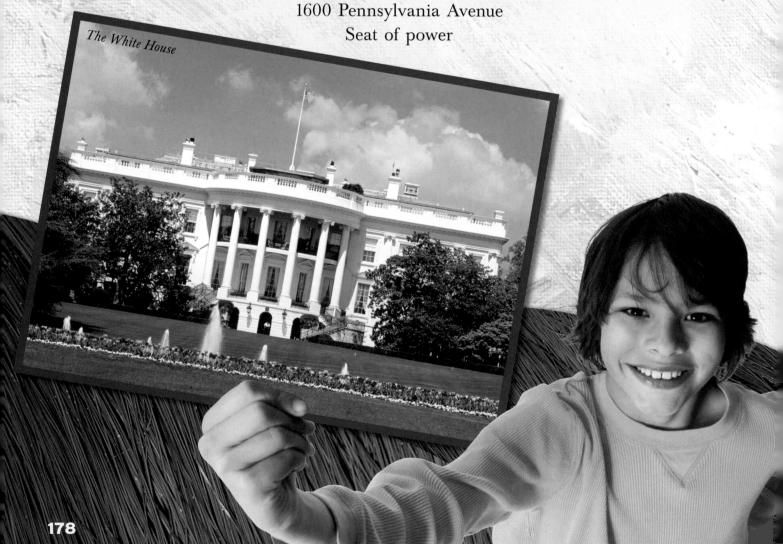

The White House

Risen from the ashes of British invaders' fire
The Capitol with its majestic dome reaching for the sky
Beckons from high on Jenkins Hill.
Congress's Workplace hosts two Senators from each state,
But Representatives by state size,
Who sponsor bills, argue, compromise
Until all conclude a bill is fair enough
To be made law.

The U.S. Capitol

The Supreme Court Building

Shouldered by sixteen marble pillars
Strong and sound as our nation's Founders,
This promise is inscribed: "Equal Justice Under Law."
The Supreme Court's nine appointed judges
Black robed and evenhanded, serve for life,
Ruling on the lawfulness of each selected case,
Guided through a tangle of competing aims
By the U.S. Constitution.

New Drama Series **CHANNEL 9 • SUNDAY**

Halls of POWER

Do you live for politics? Do the inner workings of the government fascinate you? Does watching the Senate debate absorb your attention like a good baseball game? Are you hooked on power? Then *Halls of Power* is the television show for you. This new hour-long drama will capture your attention from the opening scenes.

In the pilot program, we meet Samantha Albert. She is the tough new majority leader of the House. Within the first 10 minutes, Albert is head-to-head with the President and Senate over the budget and taxes. Albert may be tough, but she is also smart. And she's a deal maker. The show is a nice lesson on compromise in government.

All of the political players have considerable power, but the writers do a great job showing how the U.S. Constitution provides checks and balances. Each side wants to win. They bend the rules, they argue. But in the end, they have to play by the rules to get anything done.

Verbs

Activity One

About Verbs

Verbs are words that express an action or a state of being. Action verbs tell what the subject of the sentence does. Some action verbs are *tap*, *whisper*, or *flip*. State of being verbs state that something IS. Some state of being verbs are *am*, *is*, *are*, *was*, and *were*. As your teacher reads *Halls of Power*, listen for the verbs.

Verbs in Context

With a partner, read *Halls of Power* and look for the verbs. Make a chart like the one below. List all of the verbs you find and their meanings.

VERB	MEANING
live	to exist

Activity Two

Explore Words Together

Work with a partner to a write a sentence for each of the action verbs listed on the right. Share your sentences with the class.

construct	gape
exhaust	lend
furnish	scrub

Activity Three

Explore Words in Writing

Find an interesting paragraph in a book that you like. Write the paragraph on a piece of paper and circle all the verbs. Then think of other verbs that would work just as well in the sentences. Rewrite the passage using those verbs. Share your paragraph with a partner.

GUESS WHO'S *Home*

by Alice McGinty

"Come on, Isabel," Leah called. "You're behind again."

Isabel looked up from the portrait she'd been studying in the Green Room of the White House. She must have been daydreaming. Her class had already moved on to the next room of their White House tour. Isabel and Leah ran to catch up with them. They found themselves looking into a huge open room with glittering crystal chandeliers. Their teacher, Mrs. Morris, was saying to the class, "The President uses the East Room for large social gatherings and ceremonies."

Isabel peered around the other members of her fifth grade class to get a better look at the grand piano in the middle of the room. It was lovely!

Her class had come all the way from Pennsylvania to see the sights of Washington, D.C., and this tour was a highlight for Isabel. She'd always dreamed of what it might be like to live in the White House.

What strategies could you use to help you understand the importance of the East Room in the White House?

182

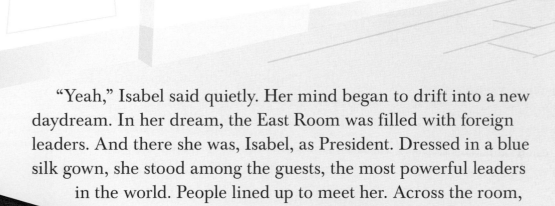

"Yeah," Isabel said quietly. Her mind began to drift into a new daydream. In her dream, the East Room was filled with foreign leaders. And there she was, Isabel, as President. Dressed in a blue silk gown, she stood among the guests, the most powerful leaders in the world. People lined up to meet her. Across the room, somebody played a waltz on the piano.

Suddenly, Isabel jerked out of her daydream and realized that the room was empty and eerily quiet. Her class had vanished. Panicked, Isabel turned and ran into the hallway to find them, frantically dashing from room to room, up and down hallways, her heart pounding. She ducked under a barricade and darted up a flight of stairs. At the top, Isabel turned a corner and started down another hallway. When she heard voices, she looked up. It took her a second to realize what she was seeing, but when she did, she stopped in her tracks.

What strategies could help you understand the events of this section?

Two-Word Technique
Write down two words that reflect your thoughts about each page. Discuss them with your partner.

"Mr. President," she whispered. He stopped, too, staring at Isabel.

"Excuse me, young lady," the President said. "May I assist you?"

"I . . . I'm lost," Isabel stammered. "I don't know where my class is."

The President's eyes softened and he stepped closer to her. "Come," he said, taking her hand. "Let's find your class."

They began to walk down the hallway, hand in hand, and Isabel couldn't help wondering if this was part of another daydream. "M . . . may I ask you a question?" she asked the President, timidly.

"Certainly," the President answered.

"What's it like being the most powerful leader in the free world? That's what my teacher says you are."

The President laughed. "Most of the time I don't feel particularly powerful, young lady," he said. Our government is a three-part balancing act between the executive, legislative, and judicial branches."

"I don't understand," Isabel said.

What could you do to help you understand the conversation between Isabel and the President?

"I'm the head of the *executive* branch of the government," the President explained. "There are many agencies in the executive branch, such as the Department of Agriculture. Our job is to run the country and carry out the federal laws. I work with the Office of Management and Budget to suggest how the government should spend its money each year. I also negotiate treaties with the powerful leaders of foreign countries."

Isabel smiled as she remembered her daydream.

"Then there is the legislative branch of the government," the President continued. "That's Congress. The people from each state elect members of Congress to represent them. I'm sure you've studied the Senate and House of Representatives. The legislative branch makes sure I don't have too much power. They don't always agree with what I say or do. If a law isn't working, they can vote to change it. You see, their job is to create laws, change laws, and get rid of any laws that don't work."

What could you do to figure out how duties of the executive and legislative branches differ?

Isabel thought about the responsibilities for a moment, and then asked, "And what's the last part of the balancing act?"

"That's the judicial branch," the President said. "Courts interpret laws and settle arguments, and if they find a law that's unconstitutional, they can overturn it. They make sure the laws work right for the people of our country."

"I think I understand," said Isabel.

"Good," said the President, "and just in time. We're taking a shortcut," he said. "We'll meet your class at the end of the tour." The next thing Isabel knew, they were walking right toward her class.

"Isabel!" Leah shouted in amazement. Then everyone looked over in shock and surprise.

"It seems you've lost a classmate," the President said. "I hope you've all enjoyed your tour of my home. While we're here, would you like to take a photograph together?"

Mrs. Morris, who'd been standing stone still in amazement, finally found her voice. "Certainly, Mr. President," she said as she lined up the class.

What strategies could you use to understand the differences between the judicial and the legislative and executive branches?

Isabel stood proudly in the center of the line next to the President, the most powerful leader in the world.

Think and Respond

Reflect and Write

- You and your partner took turns reading *Guess Who's Home.* Discuss with a partner your thoughts.

- Choose two parts you found difficult. On one side of an index card, write down what was in the text. On the other side, write down what you and your partner did to try to understand the text better.

Verbs in Context

Reread *Guess Who's Home.* to find examples of verbs. Then work with a partner to use some of the verbs in a short poem about the duties of the executive branch. Share your poem with the class.

Turn and Talk

MONITOR UNDERSTANDING

Discuss with a partner what you have learned about how to monitor understanding.

- Why is it important to monitor your understanding as you read?

- What can you do when you don't understand something you've read?

Review the unclear details you listed for *Guess Who's Home.* Discuss with your partner strategies you can use to monitor your understanding.

Critical Thinking

With a small group, brainstorm the duties of the executive, judicial, and legislative branches of our government. Review *Guess Who's Home* and record the duties of the different branches of the government. Then discuss these questions.

- How do you think having three branches of government provides a balance of power?

- What happens if one branch becomes more powerful than the other two?

Water, 1566
Giuseppe Arcimboldo (1527–1593)

Viewing

The artist who painted this picture was Giuseppe Arcimboldo. He was born in Italy in the 1500s. He is best known for painting objects so that they look like something else entirely.

1. What kinds of things do you see in the painting? What do they have in common? Why do you think the artist titled the painting *Water*?

2. When you look at all the things in the painting together, what do you see?

3. Look at the animals in the painting. How do you think their colors and patterns and shapes might fool their enemies? How would this help the animals survive in the ocean?

4. Why might an artist also use methods to fool the viewer?

In This UNIT

In this unit, you will read about animals that live in the ocean. You will learn what animals live at different ocean depths. You will also learn about how deep-sea creatures adapt to life in the ocean.

Contents

Modeled Reading

Shared Reading

Interactive Reading

BIG BLUE

by Shelley Gill • illustrated by Ann Barrow

Critical Listening

Critical listening is listening for facts and opinions. Listen to the focus questions your teacher will read to you.

Blue WHALES

Super Size

The blue whale is closely related to another **marine** animal, the **dolphin**. You wouldn't know it from their size! The blue whale is the largest animal to **inhabit** our planet. If you visit the American Museum of Natural History in Washington, D.C., you can see just how big. The museum has a life-size model hanging from its ceiling. It must have been a challenge to create this **unique** model.

 **Did You Know?** Blue whales are a kind of baleen whale. Rather than teeth, baleen whales have plates that act like strainers to separate their food from seawater. Some baleen whales eat **plankton** —tiny plants and animals that drift in the ocean. Blue whales eat tiny shrimp-like animals called krill. In the summer, a blue whale can eat more than 7 tons of krill a day. Blue whales do most of their eating during the summer. During their fall journey to warmer waters near the equator, the giant creatures eat very little.

Structured Vocabulary Discussion

Work with a partner to complete the following sentences about your vocabulary words.

Plankton is important because . . . .

You could describe yourself as *unique* because . . . .

> Throughout the week, add to your vocabulary journal entries. Record new insights and other words that relate to this week's vocabulary.

Picture It

Copy this word organizer into your vocabulary journal. Fill in the circles with places that people, plants, or animals can **inhabit**.

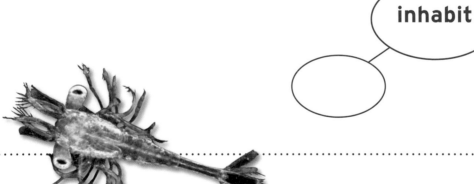

house — inhabit

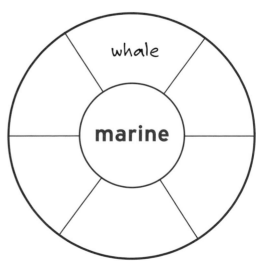

Copy this word organizer into your vocabulary journal. Fill in each section with the name of a different kind of **marine** animal.

whale — marine

Comprehension Strategy

Create Images

Creating mental images can help you understand what you read. Before you read, look at the selection's title and pictures. Do images come to mind? As you read, use your memories and five senses to create more images. After you read, think and talk about the images you created.

Create mental IMAGES as you read.

Think about how something you read might look, sound, feel, smell, and taste to create a mental image.

TURN AND TALK Listen as your teacher reads the following lines from *Big Blue*. Read the lines with a partner. Talk about the images that come to mind. Then answer the following questions.

• If you could draw a picture of Kye's dream, what would it look like?

• How do the words make you feel? Are there other things in your life that make you feel the same way?

Every night before I go to sleep, I make a wish. Someday I want to swim with a blue whale. And every night I dream of whales. In the darkness, as I swim lazily toward sleep, tiny lights appear. They skim and swirl, violet, crimson, and gold, like stars blinking, like tiny fish twinkling in an ocean of night. I imagine myself twirling through space, deep-water space.

Then, only shadows at first, they appear. My dreams are filled with huge gliding shapes, swirling in turquoise waters. Whales—blue whales.

TAKE IT WITH YOU Creating images helps you understand what you read. The process also makes reading more fun. As you read other selections, write down which senses and memories you used to create mental images. Use a chart like the one below to record your images.

In the Text

"In the darkness, as I swim lazily toward sleep, tiny lights appear. They skim and swirl, violet, crimson, and gold, like stars blinking, like tiny fish twinkling in an ocean of night. I imagine myself twirling through space, deep-water space.

Then, only shadows at first, they appear. Whales—blue whales."

Image in My Mind

I try to picture myself as the swimmer in the dream, floating in an imaginary ocean.

See

I see tiny twinkling lights in the ocean blackness.

Touch

I feel the water surrounding my body. It surges around me.

Hear

I hear the muffled sounds of the water all around me.

Smell

I smell the ocean as I come to the surface for air.

Taste

I taste the saltwater in my mouth.

Feel

I feel the excitement and awe that Kye feels when the whales appear.

Ocean Census Half Completed

by David L. Dreier

Washington, D.C.—Do you think the oceans have been explored? If you do, think again. Scientists have studied only a small part of the ocean depths. The Census of Marine Life—a massive 10-year study—hopes to change this. Project leaders recently updated reporters on the project's goals and progress.

Project Goals

The study began in 2000. It will run through 2010. Scientists from more than 70 countries are helping with the project. The study seeks to answer three questions: What lived in the ocean in the distant past? What lives there now? What will live there in the future? Some teams are using historical information to study past ocean life.

Other teams are exploring the oceans to find current information. The teams will then compare the findings. The scientists hope to answer important questions. For example, the study wants to see how fishing has affected ocean life.

Discoveries

The study has already recorded many interesting findings. One team found tiny sponges that feed on other sea creatures. Another team located huge spinning rings of plankton. One team has even found a large "dead zone" on the floor of the Indian Ocean. Divers were unable to find signs of large sea life there. Scientists believe the zone was caused by the earthquake that led to the 2004 tsunami.

Expected Benefits

Why is it important to study ocean life? The ocean is a major resource. The teams hope they will find new fishing areas. This could help ease overfishing in current areas. Project leaders also believe the teams can find thousands of new plants and animals. These plants and animals might one day be used to make useful medicines. By studying the past and present of oceans, the team hopes to make life better in the future.

NIBBLE, NIBBLE, NIBBLE

Dear Nancy,

Hello from beautiful Kona, Hawaii! I am having the greatest vacation ever! Yesterday, we had planned to go shopping, but it was too pretty a day for that. Dad decided we should go snorkeling instead. We could have snorkeled near the hotel, but Mom said she would rather go to a place she saw in the guidebook. It was worth the drive. I will always remember the experience.

I have never seen so many fish—it was totally awesome! The fish were swimming so close to me that I could hear them making little munching sounds. I must admit it was a little eerie. I would have been frightened, except the fish were pretty small. In spite of what my brother says, I don't think they were trying to eat me! My brother has definitely been reading too many science fiction stories.

We are going snorkeling again tomorrow. Dad says this time I can bring a disposable underwater camera. I can't wait to show you the pictures. This week in Hawaii is going to be great!

Love,

Alicia

Helping Verbs

Activity One

About Helping Verbs

A helping verb comes before the main verb in a sentence to tell about an action or about time. *Am*, *is*, *are*, *was*, *were*, *has*, *have*, *had*, *will*, *would*, *can*, *could*, *might*, and *should* are examples of helping verbs. Listen for the helping verbs as your teacher reads the letter.

Helping Verbs in Context

With a partner, read the letter to find the helping verbs. Make a chart like the one below. Write the helping verb in the first column. In the second column, write a short sentence using the helping verb. Share your favorite sentences with the class.

WORD	SENTENCE
is	My brother is going swimming at the beach.

Activity Two

Explore Words Together

The list on the right contains helping verbs. Work with a partner to write a sentence using each helping verb. Then pick two additional helping verbs not included in the list and write a sentence using those words.

is	were
are	has
was	had

Activity Three

Explore Words in Writing

Write your own letter about a vacation or about a water activity. Use as many helping verbs in the letter as you can. Then exchange your letter with a partner and circle all of the helping verbs.

Squid Attack!

By John Manos

Rollie felt awful. His palms were sweating, his heart was racing, and he couldn't seem to breathe. He kept thinking of that last trip into deep water. . . .

He stared down at *Izzy*, his individual submersible deep-sea vessel. He had always loved climbing into the sub's cramped interior and diving thousands of feet below the surface of the ocean. Now he could barely endure the sight of its domed top. The thought of sliding down into the steel shell and pulling the hatch closed made his knees feel weak.

Rollie used to love that moment, as the sub went down ever deeper beneath the waves, when sunlight disappeared. It was as if he were watching a competition between the world of warm sunshine and the deep, dark, icy ocean bottom. He used to think that the sunlight was winning. Ever since his last dive, he was sure that the opposite was true. The competition was uneven. The cold, deadly depths had won. *If only I could get back to Australia right now*, he thought. *I would attach myself to land like a barnacle on a pier.*

> What mental images do you have of Rollie before his dive in the submersible?

But there was no turning back. Only Rollie knew how to pilot *Izzy*. If he refused to make the dive, the entire deep-ocean science mission would be a failure. Rollie looked out over the ocean and almost smiled when he saw whales in the distance. The familiar sight reminded him of the importance of his work.

As he climbed to *Izzy's* hatch, Rollie looked around. *Is this the last time I'll feel the sun on my neck?* he wondered. Are those the last whales I will ever see? He turned his eyes to the long cable that would attach *Izzy* to the ship. "Please, please don't break," he pleaded in a whisper as he lowered himself into the tight quarters of the submersible. Rollie involuntarily gasped for breath as he heard a worker sealing the hatch. Rollie knew that during his descent to 2,000 feet below the surface and all the time he was underwater, he would be dependent on *Izzy's* air tanks. He had 72 hours of life support. Last time, that had barely been enough.

What words does the author use to help you create a mental image of the ocean?

203

Say Something Technique
Take turns reading a section of text, covering it up, and then saying something about it to your partner. You may say any thought or idea that the text brings to your mind.

Rollie checked the submersible's control panel to make sure his microphone was turned off, then he sighed heavily. "Come on, Rollie," he said aloud. "Get a grip on yourself. You've done this dozens of times—one bad experience doesn't change all the others."

"Are you connected, Rollie?" Hiro's voice came over the speaker. Hiro was the research scientist in charge of today's dive. He was the only person on board who knew what had happened to Rollie on his last dive, six months ago. "Let me hear you, pal," Hiro said, with a slight concern in his voice.

Rollie flipped the microphone switch, reluctantly. "I'm here," he answered. Rollie felt the familiar jolt as he dropped toward the water. He watched the water rise up to meet him, then surround him, and then cover the dome of the sub. The surface light became dim and then disappeared altogether. Rollie was warm inside *Izzy*, but he knew that just inches from his face was water too cold for him to survive. The pressure outside his protective sub would have crushed him like a paper cup.

How does the text give you a mental picture of Rollie as he sinks below the surface?

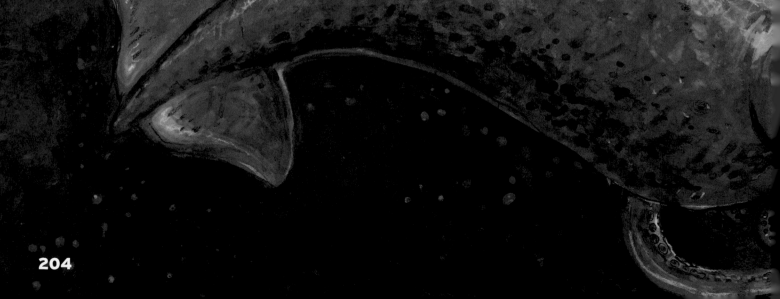

204

Rollie glanced up, but no surface light was visible. Looking back down into the beam from his headlights, he suddenly screamed. Sweeping toward him was a giant squid! Its tentacles surrounded the sub. Rollie suddenly felt as if he were back on his last dive. At that time, *Izzy* had been tangled in cables from the deep-water shipwreck Rollie was exploring. At the memory, Rollie began to panic.

"What? What's happening?" Hiro cried, but Rollie couldn't answer. Rollie saw steel cables instead of the squid's tentacles and was terrified at being trapped again far below the surface. He felt sharp tugs on the submersible as he desperately tried to free himself now. Another scream burst from Rollie's throat.

Hiro used the remote to turn on the sub's cameras as Rollie began to whisper frantically. "Trapped," his hoarse voice said. "I'm trapped on the sunken ship, and my air is running out."

"No!" Hiro shouted, "You have three days of air!" All Hiro heard in reply was a long, shuddering moan from Rollie. "The submersible isn't tangled in the cables of a sunken ship, Rollie," Hiro went on. "It's only a squid!"

What mental image do you have that helps you understand Rollie's feelings?

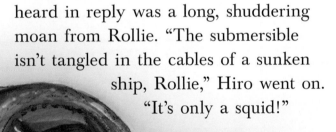

"Only a squid?" Rollie groaned. Then he gasped when he saw the giant squid's beak opening and closing in the lights; another wave of terror shook Rollie's entire body. One of the squid's long arms was wrapped around the submersible's dome, its double rows of suckers gripping the glass. Rollie screamed again. He could see the squid's huge black eye and feeding tentacles that were more than 40 feet long.

At last Rollie felt rage and determination replace the terror in his mind. He refused to end his life as a meal for a giant squid! Rollie grabbed the submersible's controls and tried to move away from the squid. At that moment, Rollie felt a hard, sudden jerk. He saw a long row of teeth in a giant jaw as the squid released the submersible and a huge flipper flashed past. Dimly, Rollie could see an ancient competition beginning as a whale and the squid locked together in battle.

Rollie lost sight of the contest as he called to Hiro, "I'm free! I'm getting out of here!"

What mental image have you created of the squid attack?

Think and Respond

Reflect and Write

- You and your partner have read sections of *Squid Attack!* Discuss the ideas you formed in response to the story.

- Choose two mental images you created while you read. On one side of an index card, write the page numbers of the images. On the other side of the index card, sketch the image or describe it.

Helping Verbs in Context

Reread *Squid Attack!* to find examples of helping verbs. Write down the words you find. Include the helping verbs in a paragraph describing a mental image you had while reading the story. Share your paragraph with a partner.

Turn and Talk

CREATE IMAGES

Discuss with a partner what you have learned so far about creating images.

- What does it mean to create mental images?

- How do you create images in your mind as you read?

Choose one of the mental images you created while reading *Squid Attack!* Explain to a partner how that image helped you enjoy and understand the story.

Critical Thinking

With a partner, brainstorm reasons that people become terrified. Write your list on a sheet of paper. Look back at *Squid Attack!* Write what happened to Rollie on his previous dive. Write on the other side of the page why Rollie was afraid of going back underwater. Then answer these questions.

- Why do you think Rollie was willing to go on another dive?

- Was Rollie's reaction to the giant squid a reasonable reaction? Why or why not?

- What caused him to react the way he did?

Deep Sea Monsters

Movie Review

Documentary movie, 82 minutes, Rated G

Do you ever wonder what lives at the bottom of the ocean? Just **attach** a camera to a robot submarine and see for yourself. That is what the makers of *Deep Sea Monsters* did.

The main **section** of the movie is about the life forms that live around hot vents deep in the Atlantic and Pacific Oceans. Hot vents are like underwater hot springs. Some of the life forms that have adapted to these high temperatures are huge. The movie highlights 6-foot-long worms. Others are small, like the blind shrimp that swarm around the hot vents in **competition** for food.

The movie gives us an up-close look at the tiniest life forms in this ocean zone, too. Some ocean bacteria contain **chlorophyll**. This lets the bacteria absorb light to produce energy. The bacteria living near the hot vents use chemicals in the water instead of sunlight to make energy.

The movie was fun to watch. I even learned some new things, like which sea animals have skeletons made of **cartilage** instead of bone. Want to know the answer? Watch the movie and find out for yourself.

Structured Vocabulary Discussion

When your teacher says a vocabulary word, your small group will take turns saying the first word you think of. After a few seconds, your teacher will say "Stop." The last person in your group who said a word should explain how that word is related to the vocabulary word your teacher started with.

Throughout the week, add to your vocabulary journal entries. Record new insights and other words that relate to this week's vocabulary.

Picture It

Copy this word organizer into your vocabulary journal. Fill in the blanks with things that you can use to **attach** things.

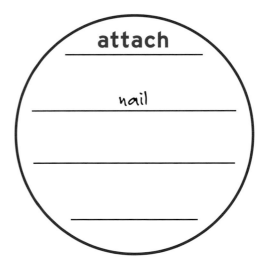

attach

_____

nail

_____

_____

_____

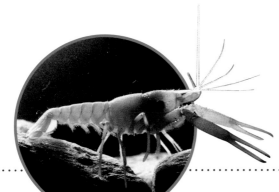

Copy this word organizer into your vocabulary journal. Fill in the sections of the circle with words that mean the same thing as **competition**.

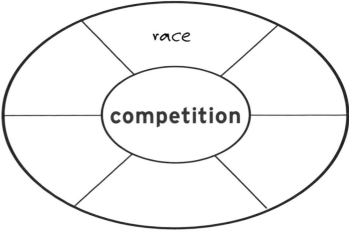

race

competition

Into the Deep

by Abby Jones

sunlit waves winking

twinkling rays streaming,

sinking

down below

through reds and golds

warming life that swims and grows

inviting those from humbler zones to dine

'til time

calls them down . . .

down . . .

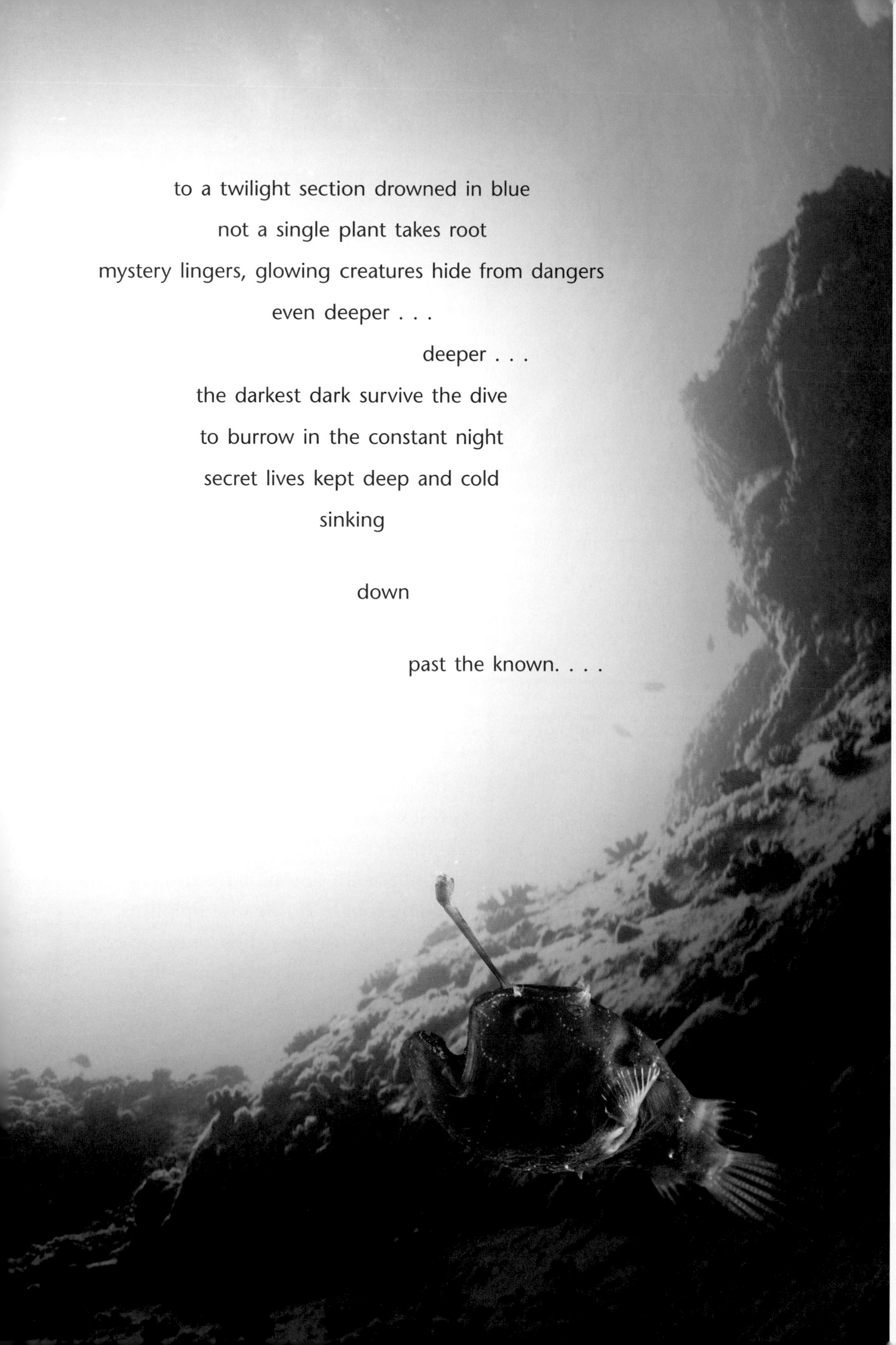

to a twilight section drowned in blue

not a single plant takes root

mystery lingers, glowing creatures hide from dangers

even deeper . . .

deeper . . .

the darkest dark survive the dive

to burrow in the constant night

secret lives kept deep and cold

sinking

down

past the known. . . .

All About DOLPHINS

Tale of the Teeth

Dolphins are part of the whale family. Unlike blue whales and other baleen whales, dolphins are toothed whales. A dolphin's teeth are cone-shaped and very sharp. Dolphins use their sharp teeth to catch slippery fish and other prey. Some dolphins eat only fish. Other dolphins seem to prefer a diet of squid and octopus. Bottlenose dolphins are fond of fish, mollusks, and crabs and other crustaceans.

Did you Know?

Unlike humans and most other mammals, a dolphin's skin is thick and hairless. The dolphin's skin feels smooth to the touch. A dolphin's skin doesn't have time to become rough. Bottlenose dolphins, for instance, replace their outer layer of skin every two hours! Smooth skin helps the dolphin move quickly through the water.

Super Stars!

Dolphins are playful and very smart. The animals often seem as though they are having fun. Dolphins are able to quickly learn tricks and imitate actions. Some dolphins have even become television and movie actors!

Linking Verbs

Activity One

About the Linking Verbs

Linking verbs are verbs that connect the subject in a sentence to a noun or an adjective in the predicate part of the sentence. *Am*, *is*, *are*, *was*, *were*, *been*, *become*, *feels*, *look*, *smell*, and *seems* are examples of linking verbs. As your teacher reads *All About Dolphins*, listen for the linking verbs.

Linking Verbs

With a partner, read *All About Dolphins*. Find the sentences that contain linking verbs. For each sentence you find, write the subject in the first column, the linking verb in the second column, and what the verb links in the third column.

SUBJECT	LINKING VERB	WHAT IT LINKS
dolphin's skin	feels	smooth

Activity Two

Explore Words Together

The list on the right contains six linking verbs. Work with a partner to create sentences using the words.

is	become
are	seem
was	feel

Activity Three

Explore Words in Writing

Many words can be linking verbs. Write a short letter to a friend describing some of the things you have learned about dolphins. Use at least 5 linking verbs. If you want, you may use four verbs from the list above. Share your letter with a partner.

DR. Sylvia Earle

by Mary Dylewski

Sylvia Earle once joked that a wave swept her into the ocean when she was three years old and that she has loved the sea ever since! Her love of the water turned into a career. She became a deep-sea scientist. Today, Dr. Earle studies some of the millions of creatures that live in the oceans. In addition to her studies, Dr. Earle has another goal. She wants everyone to know how important it is to protect the oceans that cover much of our planet.

Until she was a young teen, Sylvia Earle lived on a small farm in New Jersey. In summer her family often went to the shore. Earle fondly recalls these trips. She remembers on the way there first being able to smell the ocean and then hearing the water pound against the shore. After a few more minutes, she would finally see the water she loves so much.

What details tell you when Dr. Earle first discovered that she loved the sea?

As if it were a dream come true, Earle's family moved to Florida when she was a teen. There, Earle recalls spending many days after school wandering along the beach. She watched crabs run along the sand. She saw fish swim through the currents. Earle also recalls using a small faceplate, or mask, to watch starfish moving sluggishly along the ocean floor. Unfortunately, the faceplate let her stay underwater only for as long as she could hold her breath.

How do the details here help you form a new idea about Dr. Earle as a teen?

Earle's first real dive took place when she was 18. She and some other students used scuba tanks to explore the waters off Florida. Earle was thrilled that she could be underwater and breathe! She could stay there for a much longer time than she could with a just a mask. It was probably then that Earle decided to study the ocean's plants and animals.

In college Dr. Earle studied ocean life. At the time, she focused on marine plants, because plants play such an important role in any living system. Plants use chlorophyll to make their own food. Plants also provide food for other organisms.

Read, Cover, Remember, Retell Technique
With a partner, take turns reading as much text as you can cover with your hand. Then cover up what you read and retell the information to your partner.

Dr. Earle is interested in all aspects of ocean life. She once lived in a small structure in the ocean for two weeks! The underwater home even had a living room with a television. No one really watched it, according to Dr. Earle. She claims the best show was happening outside. Dr. Earle recalls not wanting to sleep, so she could spend more time in the water with the brightly colored fish.

Dr. Earle also helped organize several trips to study humpback whales. She and her team did more than observe the whales from the deck of a boat. They spent time in the water as the whales danced like ballerinas around them. Dr. Earle recalls one of the whales being so close that she could have reached out and touched its sleek skin.

What new idea do you have about Dr. Earle based on the details here?

1964

Earle is one of 70 scientists—and the only woman—who set off for six weeks to explore the Indian Ocean.

1970

Earle spends two weeks living 50 feet below sea level studying fish and other reef organisms.

1977

Earle lives on a boat for three months to study humpback whales near Hawaii.

1979

Earle dives to 1,250 feet off the coast of Hawaii using a special diving suit called the Jim Suit.

1960   **1970**   **1980**

In 1979, Dr. Earle was strapped to the front of a small submarine and taken down to 1,250 feet off the coast of Hawaii. To explore this part of the ocean, Earle wore a 1000-pound suit. She claims the suit made her look like a huge white bear! During her dive Dr. Earle came face-to-face with a small shark. Unlike other fish, a shark has no bones. Instead, its skeleton is made of a tough, elastic material called cartilage. As Earle watched the shark, she remembers it watched her, too, with its bright green eyes.

Dr. Earle has spent more than 6,000 hours diving in the ocean. This has made her realize that without water, there can be no life. As a result, Dr. Earle has undertaken another mission— to save Earth's oceans.

What do you learn after reading this page that helps you know something new about Dr. Earle's work?

1998

1985

Earle uses a submersible named Deep Rover to set a record of 3,281 feet for a solo dive by a woman.

Earle is named a hero for planet Earth and becomes an explorer-in-residence at the National Geographic Society.

1990   **2000**

Dr. Earle knows that all plants and animals in the ocean play important roles. She also knows that a change in any group causes changes in other groups. These changes also affect the ocean. For Dr. Earle, the answer is to protect the oceans.

Dr. Earle feels that too many people look only at the ocean's surface and see just water. She wants people to look below the surface. Dr. Earle wants people to get into the water. She wants them to look at the plants and animals that call the ocean home. And then she wants people to take responsibility for protecting that home.

Based on the details about Dr. Earle, what do you think she wants people to do concerning the ocean?

Think and Respond

Reflect and Write

- You and your partner took turns retelling sections of *Dr. Sylvia Earle* as you read. Discuss your retellings.

- On one side of an index card, write one statement that synthesizes information from the biography. On the other side of the card, list the pieces of information that went into your synthesis.

Linking Verbs in Context

Reread *Dr. Sylvia Earle* to find examples of linking verbs. Write down the words you find. Use the words in a short poem about studying ocean life. Share your sentences with a partner.

Turn and Talk

SYNTHESIZE

Discuss with a partner what you have learned so far about synthesizing what you read.

- What does it mean to synthesize?

- How do you synthesize information?

Choose one of the syntheses you created for a section of *Dr. Sylvia Earle*. Compare your synthesis with that of a partner. Are your syntheses similar? If not, how do they differ?

Critical Thinking

In a group, discuss reasons why oceans are important to study. Write your ideas on one side of a sheet of paper. Return to *Dr. Sylvia Earle*. Write reasons Dr. Earle believes we should study the ocean. Then answer these questions.

- How do you think Dr. Earle's experiences as a teenager helped prepare her to study ocean life as an adult?

- Why might studying ocean plants have helped Dr. Earle better understand sea animals?

Contents

Bottom of the Deep Blue Sea

DOWN, DOWN, DOWN IN THE OCEAN

by Sandra Markle
illustrated by Bob Marstall

Appreciative Listening

Appreciative listening is listening for language that helps you create a picture in your mind. Listen to the focus questions your teacher will read to you.

Adapting to the DEEP

The ocean is a huge and challenging **environment**. Many fish compete with one another for food. If fish aren't big or fast, they need another way to escape from hungry enemies. Some fish protect themselves by blending in with their surroundings in the **niche**, or special habitat, in which they live.

Hatchet Fish The hatchet fish has a thin, ax-blade body. This shape combined with its silver color makes the fish hard to see against the lighted ocean surface. The hatchet fish also has a row of lights along its belly. These lights add to the **camouflage**. Food is scarce in the deep ocean. Like many deep-sea fish, hatchet fish **conserve** energy by waiting for their prey to come to them.

Salps A salp hides from its enemies by being almost **transparent**. A clear body is hard to see, particularly if that body is small. Many salps are less than 4 inches long!

Structured Vocabulary Discussion

Work with a partner to complete the following sentences about your vocabulary words.

_____ is to *habitat* as *state* is to *country*.

Use is to _____ as *empty* is to *full*.

> Throughout the week, add to your vocabulary journal entries. Record new insights and other words that relate to this week's vocabulary.

Picture It

Copy this word organizer into your vocabulary journal. Fill in the boxes with examples of ways you could **camouflage** yourself in different places.

camouflage

I could wear green and brown in a forest.

Copy this word organizer into your vocabulary journal. Fill in the ovals with words that describe **transparent**, and list examples of things that are transparent in the boxes.

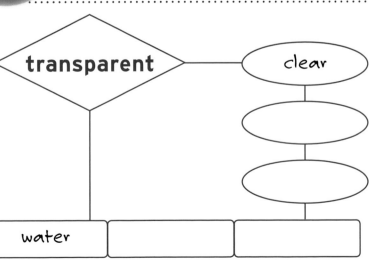

transparent

clear

water

Use Fix-Up Strategies

Using fix-up strategies is a way to solve problems when you read. If you have trouble reading a page or get stuck on a word or sentence, first think about the problem. Then decide what you can do to help fix the problem. You may read on for meaning, or use other fix-up strategies to help you understand.

FIX-UP STRATEGIES help when you get stuck on a word.

When you get stuck on a word, try different strategies to help you figure it out.

TURN AND TALK Listen to your teacher read the following lines from *Down, Down, Down in the Ocean*. Then with a partner, read the following lines from the story. Discuss the fix-up strategies you can use to help you solve any problems with the text.

• Were you able to read the passage without stopping?

• What strategy did you use to help you continue reading and understanding?

A salp drifts, suspended in the deep, blue water. Transparent, like molded clear gelatin, it is a ghostly hunter. By ambushing prey instead of searching for it, a salp conserves energy—important where food is scarce.

Longer than a school bus, a salp looks like a giant sea creature. In fact, it is a colony of transparent animals clinging together to stay safe and share food energy.

TAKE IT WITH YOU Using fix-up strategies will help you understand what you read. As you read other selections, determine the problems you face and choose the appropriate fix-up strategy. Use a chart like the one below to help you with the process.

Word I Got Stuck On	What I Did				Which One Worked?
	Used Illustrations	Used Phonics	Read On	Broke It into Parts	
transparent	✓	✓	✔	✓	I read on and got an idea of what the word means from the words and phrases around it, such as "clear" and "ghostly."

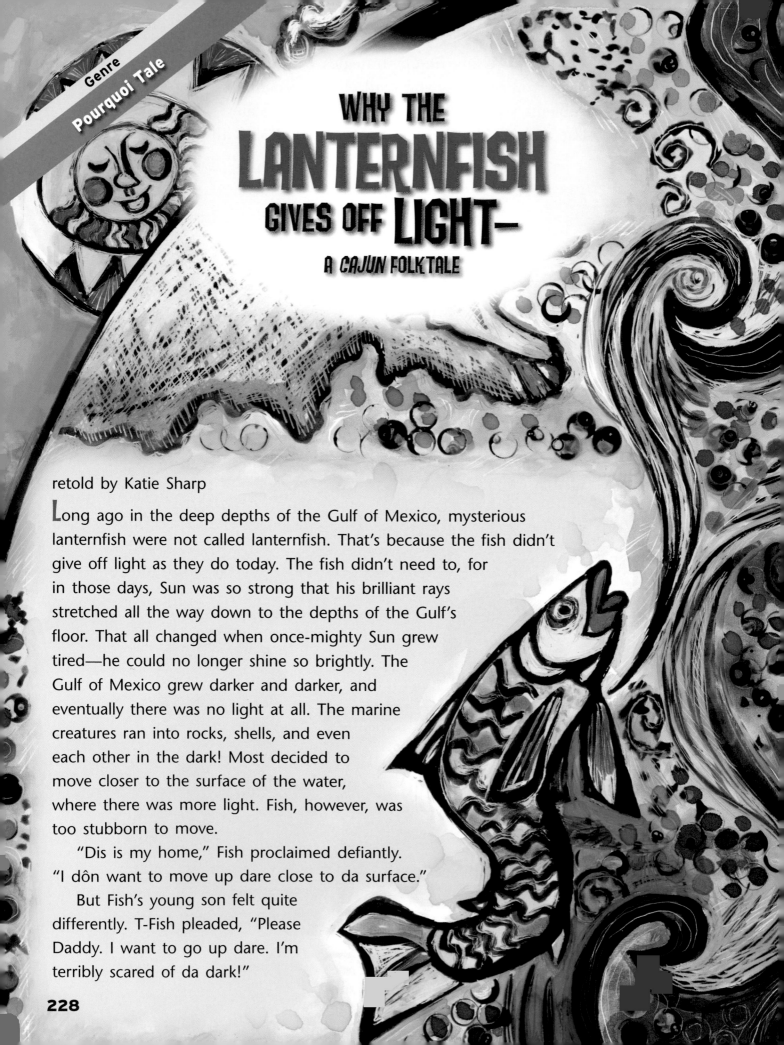

WHY THE LANTERNFISH GIVES OFF LIGHT—

A CAJUN FOLKTALE

retold by Katie Sharp

Long ago in the deep depths of the Gulf of Mexico, mysterious lanternfish were not called lanternfish. That's because the fish didn't give off light as they do today. The fish didn't need to, for in those days, Sun was so strong that his brilliant rays stretched all the way down to the depths of the Gulf's floor. That all changed when once-mighty Sun grew tired—he could no longer shine so brightly. The Gulf of Mexico grew darker and darker, and eventually there was no light at all. The marine creatures ran into rocks, shells, and even each other in the dark! Most decided to move closer to the surface of the water, where there was more light. Fish, however, was too stubborn to move.

"Dis is my home," Fish proclaimed defiantly. "I dôn want to move up dare close to da surface."

But Fish's young son felt quite differently. T-Fish pleaded, "Please Daddy. I want to go up dare. I'm terribly scared of da dark!"

228

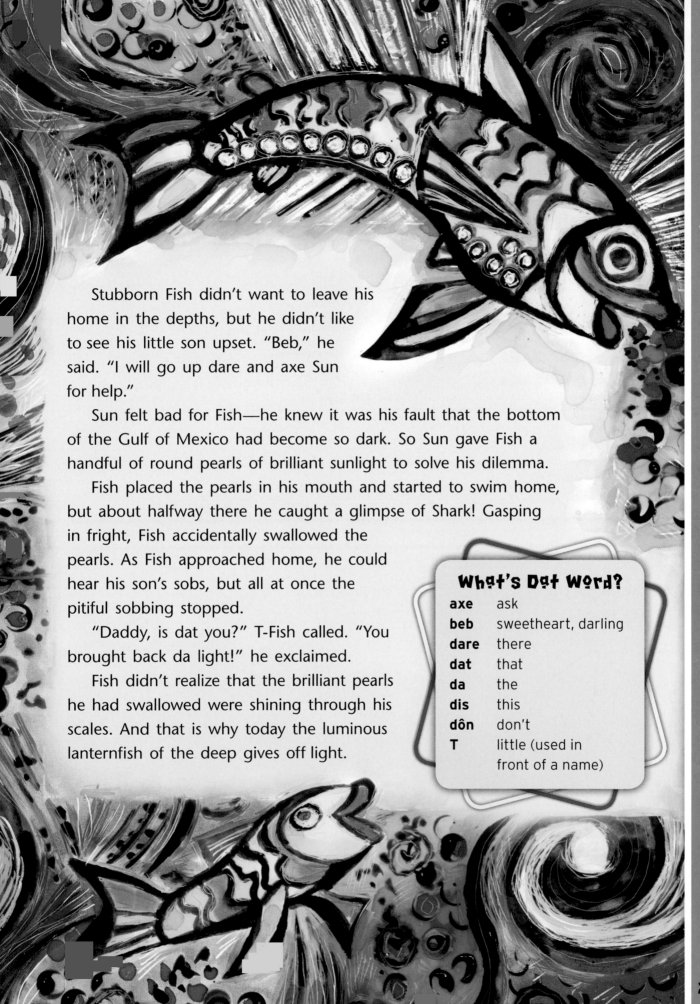

Stubborn Fish didn't want to leave his home in the depths, but he didn't like to see his little son upset. "Beb," he said. "I will go up dare and axe Sun for help."

Sun felt bad for Fish—he knew it was his fault that the bottom of the Gulf of Mexico had become so dark. So Sun gave Fish a handful of round pearls of brilliant sunlight to solve his dilemma.

Fish placed the pearls in his mouth and started to swim home, but about halfway there he caught a glimpse of Shark! Gasping in fright, Fish accidentally swallowed the pearls. As Fish approached home, he could hear his son's sobs, but all at once the pitiful sobbing stopped.

"Daddy, is dat you?" T-Fish called. "You brought back da light!" he exclaimed.

Fish didn't realize that the brilliant pearls he had swallowed were shining through his scales. And that is why today the luminous lanternfish of the deep gives off light.

What's Dat Word?

axe	ask
beb	sweetheart, darling
dare	there
dat	that
da	the
dis	this
dôn	don't
T	little (used in front of a name)

229

CREATURES of the DEEP

Dear Diary,

Last night I dreamed that my hands glowed in the dark. I'm sure it was because of yesterday's field trip to the aquarium. We watched a widescreen movie about fish that live in the dark reaches of the ocean. The movie was absolutely awesome!

The movie talked about dragonfish, which are pretty weird-looking. With their long teeth and big mouths, the fish look like monsters from the deep. Dragonfish have lights along their undersides. The light comes from photophores, little light-producing organs in the fish's bodies.

I liked the squid and the anglerfish the best. The squid shoots glowing ink at its enemies. The ink contains light-producing bacteria. The spooky anglerfish has a light dangling from its head. The light looks like a lure on the end of a fishing pole. It's like the anglerfish is fishing for other fish for dinner—now that's extremely weird!

Goodnight,

Tisha

Inflected Endings -*ed*, -*ing*, and -*s*

Activity One

About Inflected Endings

An inflected ending is a word part added to the end of a root word that changes the word in some way. Examples of inflected endings are -*ed*, -*ing*, and -*s*. You may have to change the spelling of the root word when you add an inflected ending. Note that with some words, you must add -*es* rather than just -*s*. As your teacher reads the diary entry, listen for words with inflected endings.

Inflected Endings in Context

Read *Creatures of the Deep* and make a list of all the words with inflected endings. Create a chart like the one following. Write down each word, its meaning, and the root of the word.

WORD	MEANING	ROOT
producing	making	produce

Activity Two

Explore Words Together

With a partner, think of as many words as you can that can be made into new words with all of the endings -*ed*, -*ing*, and -*s* (or -*es*). Use the words listed at the right to get started.

absorb	flee
benefit	hum
challenge	magnify

Activity Three

Explore Words in Writing

Use some of the words you listed in Activities One and Two to write five sentences about deep-sea animals. Share your sentences with a partner. Have your partner find and circle the words with inflected endings.

The Mariana TRENCH

by Elise Oliver

Earth is an amazing place. You may have heard about Earth's scorching hot deserts and polar ice caps. You may have read stories about the prairies and rainforests. You may have seen pictures of towering mountains such as Mount Everest. Maybe you have even visited deep, rocky canyons such as the Grand Canyon. But did you know that the deepest, darkest place on Earth is actually beneath the Pacific Ocean?

Under the Pacific Ocean, there is a huge canyon called the Mariana Trench. This canyon looks like a huge crack in the ocean floor. The trench is more than 1,580 miles long and has an average width of 43 miles. There is a place in the Mariana Trench that has a depth of about 36,000 feet. That's almost seven miles straight down! This canyon contains the deepest known point in the world.

What does *depth* mean? What fix-up strategies can you use to help figure out the definition?

To imagine the trench, close your eyes in a dark room. The canyon is so deep under the water that sunlight can't reach it. Inside the trench it is completely dark and bitterly cold. In fact, the temperature of the water is just above freezing.

So how did such a huge canyon form at the bottom of the Pacific Ocean? It took scientists many years to answer this question. The depth of the Mariana Trench was first measured in 1899. Since then, scientists have learned a lot about what happens under the Earth's surface.

The continents and oceans are sitting on extremely large areas of rock called "plates," such as the Philippine Plate and the Pacific Plate. These plates can be up to 200 miles thick. The plates float on hot liquid rock, called "magma." Since the continents and oceans are on top of the plates, the shape of the land and water changes as the plates move.

Look at the diagram. How can the diagram help you understand how a canyon forms in the ocean?

Cross-Section of The Mariana Trench

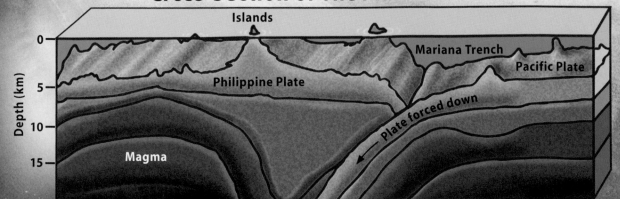

Islands

Mariana Trench

Pacific Plate

Philippine Plate

Plate forced down

Magma

Depth (km)

0

5

10

15

Reverse Think-Aloud Technique
Listen as your partner reads part of the text aloud. Choose a point in the text to stop your partner and ask what he or she is thinking about the text at that moment. Then switch roles with your partner.

The plates have been moving very slowly for billions of years. In fact, they are moving today. Plates can slide next to each other, move apart, or push together. Sometimes, there are forces that can cause one plate to be pushed over the edge of another plate. When the lower plate is driven downward, a deep trench or canyon forms. The Mariana Trench was made when two plates pushed together, and one plate was pushed over the edge of another.

Because it is so dark and cold, the Mariana Trench is a very harsh environment for living things. There are animals that can live in dark, cold conditions. But what happens when cold conditions suddenly become very hot? There are vents in the trench that shoot out extremely hot water. The temperature of the water around the vents can go from 36°F to more than 500°F in just a few seconds. Water starts to boil when it reaches 212°F!

The word *conditions* can mean many different things. How does the text help you understand what *conditions* means in this context?

There is a lot of pressure near the ocean floor because of all the water that sits on top. The water pressure inside the Mariana Trench is about eight tons per square inch. Imagine if a large elephant could balance all of its weight on a stack of quarters.

Angler Fish

The pressure on the quarters would be less than the water pressure on all sides of an object or creature in the trench.

Believe it or not, there are animals living inside the Mariana Trench. In fact, the trench has its own ecosystem. You would think that because there is no sunlight, plants could not grow. However, this is not true. The hot water that shoots out of the vents is rich in chemicals and minerals. These chemicals and minerals provide food for plants and bacteria. These plants and bacteria are at the bottom of a food chain, supporting animal life such as worms, shrimp, fish, and crabs.

How can you use the sentences in the paragraph to figure out what an *ecosystem* is?

The angler fish is one kind of animal that lives in the Mariana Trench. This strange-looking fish has its own light source. The angler fish has special chemicals inside its body that cause a bulb on its head to glow. The glow attracts smaller fish, and the angler fish swallows them when they come near its mouth.

The Mariana Trench is the deepest known point on Earth. This makes the Pacific Ocean the deepest of the planet's five oceans. But all of Earth's oceans are very deep. Scientists have found one part of the Atlantic Ocean that is about 28,000 feet deep. Future studies may find even deeper spots. The graph on this page compares the current known depths of the world's five oceans.

According to the bar graph, which ocean is the least deep?

Lantern Fish

Deepest Measurements of the World's Oceans

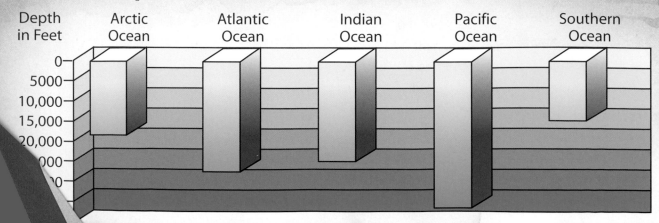

Think and Respond

Reflect and Write

• You and your partner took turns reading *The Mariana Trench*. Discuss the thoughts you had while you read.

• On one side of an index card, write down one word or idea in the selection that you had difficulty understanding. On the other side of the index card, explain what fix-up strategy helped you understand the text.

Inflected Endings in Context

Reread *The Mariana Trench* to find examples of words with the endings *-ed*, *-ing*, and *-s* or *-es*. Then use some of the words to write a paragraph about the Mariana Trench. Exchange your paragraph with a partner and circle each of the inflected endings in your partner's paragraph.

Turn and Talk

USE FIX-UP STRATEGIES

Discuss with a partner what you have learned so far about fix-up strategies.

• What is a fix-up strategy?

• What are some examples of fix-up strategies?

• How do you use fix-up strategies?

Choose one problem you had while reading *The Mariana Trench*. Explain to a partner what fix-up strategy you used to solve the problem.

Critical Thinking

Scientists look at the ways plants and animals have adapted to harsh environments on Earth, such as deserts or polar regions. In a group, make a list of characteristics that could make a place a harsh environment. Then return to *The Mariana Trench* and answer these questions.

• How have plants and animals adapted to conditions in the Mariana Trench?

• How is the Mariana Trench similar to or different from other harsh environments?

FACE TO FACE WITH A FOSSIL

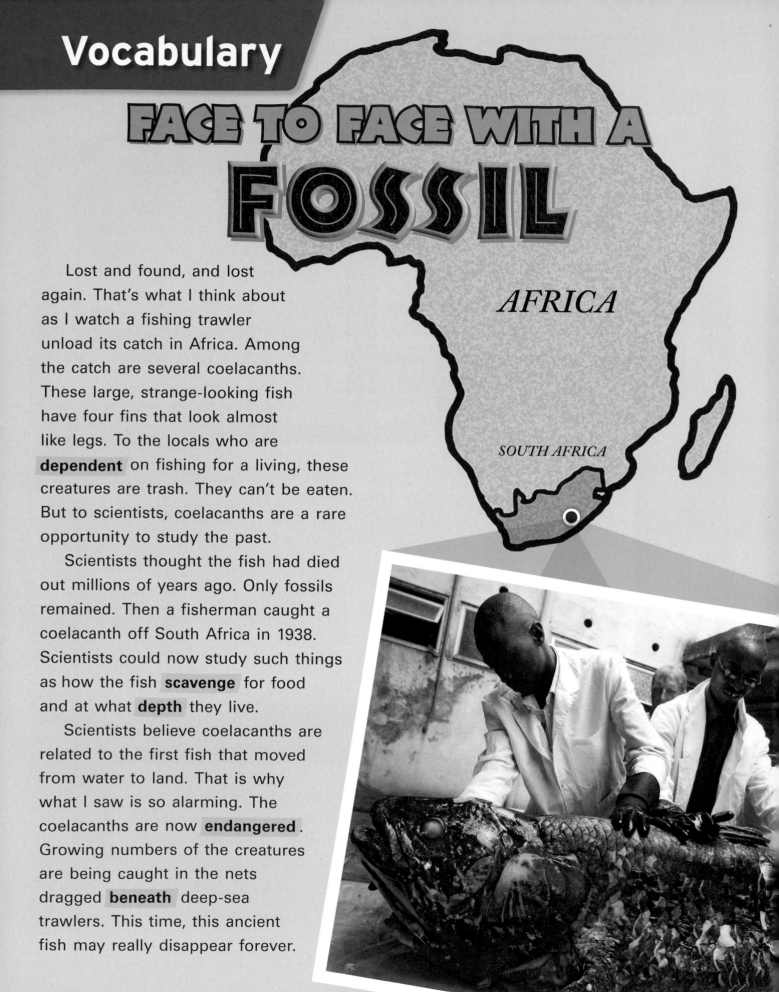

AFRICA

SOUTH AFRICA

Lost and found, and lost again. That's what I think about as I watch a fishing trawler unload its catch in Africa. Among the catch are several coelacanths. These large, strange-looking fish have four fins that look almost like legs. To the locals who are **dependent** on fishing for a living, these creatures are trash. They can't be eaten. But to scientists, coelacanths are a rare opportunity to study the past.

Scientists thought the fish had died out millions of years ago. Only fossils remained. Then a fisherman caught a coelacanth off South Africa in 1938. Scientists could now study such things as how the fish **scavenge** for food and at what **depth** they live.

Scientists believe coelacanths are related to the first fish that moved from water to land. That is why what I saw is so alarming. The coelacanths are now **endangered**. Growing numbers of the creatures are being caught in the nets dragged **beneath** deep-sea trawlers. This time, this ancient fish may really disappear forever.

Structured Vocabulary Discussion

Work with a partner to review all of your vocabulary words. Then classify as many words as you can into three categories: (1) something a fish can be, (2) something a fish can do, or (3) somewhere a fish can be. When you are finished, share your ideas with the class. Be sure to explain why you put each word in the category you did and whether any words fit into more than one category.

Throughout the week, add to your vocabulary journal entries. Record new insights and other words that relate to this week's vocabulary.

Picture It

Copy this word web into your vocabulary journal. Fill in the circles with things that have **depth**.

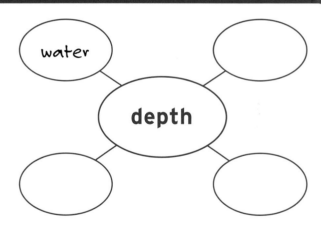

Copy this word wheel into your vocabulary journal. Fill in the sections of the circle with the names of things that can be **endangered**.

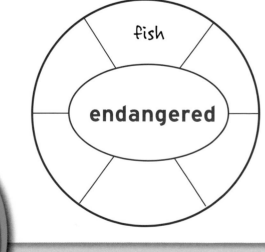

Going, Going, Gone?

by Ann Weil

I dreamed I swam with an endangered eel.
Its body was like a snake
and it swam like a fish.
Going, going, gone . . . .

I dreamed I swam with an endangered hake.
Its blue-black body
was like the midnight sky.
Going, going, gone . . . .

I dreamed I swam with an endangered
grenadier.
It had circles around its eyes
like the layers of an onion.
Going, going, gone . . . .

I saw a huge net coming at me
like a giant hand.
"Look out!" I cried aloud
and woke myself up.
Going, going, gone . . . .

I dreamed
I grew up
and swam like a fish
back down deep in the ocean.

There was no eel.
There was no hake.
There was no grenadier.
Going, going, gone . . . .

The Ribbonlike OARFISH

Location: Tropical and temperate waters worldwide

Description: The oarfish is the longest bony fish in the ocean. The fish has a sleek, silvery body. One of the oarfish's most striking features is the red crest that runs along its entire back. Long red rays with oar-like ends sprout from the fish's short bluish head. The oarfish has a small, toothless mouth, which it uses to strain small shellfish from seawater for food.

The ribbonlike oarfish can grow to be very large. The fish may even reach a length of 26 feet. However, scientists are not sure just how large this fish can actually get. The silvery beauty lives in the deep sea and comes to the ocean surface only when it is sick or dying.

Adaptation: The oarfish's red coloring helps protect it. Red is difficult to see in the deep ocean. Red coloring in an animal often acts as a signal of danger. This may encourage predators to avoid the oarfish when its red coloring is visible. Scientists believe the fish also uses its great size as protection.

Adjectives

Activity One

About Adjectives

Adjectives are words that describe nouns or pronouns. Adjectives answer one of the three questions: *What kind? How many? Which one?* In the sentence "The fish has a sleek body," *sleek* is an adjective that describes the noun *body*. *Sleek* answers the question *What kind of fish's body?* As your teacher reads the guidebook, listen for the adjectives.

Adjectives in Context

With a partner, reread the guidebook about oarfish. Enter each adjective you find in a chart like the one below. Sort the adjectives according to which question the adjective answers.

WHAT KIND?	HOW MANY?	WHICH ONE?
sleek	26	this

Activity Two

Explore Words Together

The list on the right contains nouns. Write an adjective to describe each noun. Choose at least one adjective that answers each question: What Kind? How Many? Which One? Share what you write with a partner.

oarfish   sailor

ocean   swimmer

scientist   monster

Activity Three

Explore Words in Writing

Write a paragraph using at least three of the adjective/noun pairs you created for Activity Two. Use additional nouns and adjectives as needed. Exchange your paragraph with a partner and circle the adjectives.

The Adventures of HERCULES on Sea and Land

retold by Claire Daniel

King Eurystheus (EE-you-REES-the-us) challenged the great Hercules to perform superhuman labors. Ten times Hercules was successful. Still, the king asked Hercules to perform one more task.

"You must bring me golden apples from the garden of Zeus," the king ordered. Zeus was the king of the gods. Hercules was the son of Zeus, but Hercules' mother was a mortal woman.

Hercules was stunned at the king's demand. Hera, queen of the gods, had hated Hercules even before he was born. When Hercules was a baby, Hera had put two serpents in his crib. Even then, Hercules had been so strong that he strangled the snakes.

Hera had given Zeus the golden apples as a gift. She would never let Hercules take any of them. Besides, a dragon with one hundred heads guarded the garden. The daughters of Atlas, the titan who held up the sky and Earth, also watched the apples.

What mental images do you have when you read about Hercules?

Hercules's first problem was that he didn't know the exact location of the tree that grew the golden apples. So Hercules sought the advice of the sea god Nereus (NEAR-e-us). Hercules knew this sea god was powerful and all knowing, so he treated him with great respect.

"Nereus," Hercules said, "None is mightier than you. You are the mightiest of sea gods who protect those who make their living in the sea. You have the power to aid those who are in great danger in storms and advise them of safe passages and routes. Great is the work you do for all mankind."

Nereus was not flattered by Hercules sweet-sounding words. He said, "Everyone knows of my greatness. What does the unworthy son of Zeus want from me?"

"It is a small thing," Hercules said. "I merely need to know the location of my father's garden where the golden apples grow."

Nereus sneered, "Of course I know where the garden is, but I'll never tell you. I am dependent on the friendship of Hera, and she would never forgive me if I gave you even a hint of the location."

What mental image do you have when you read about Nereus?

245

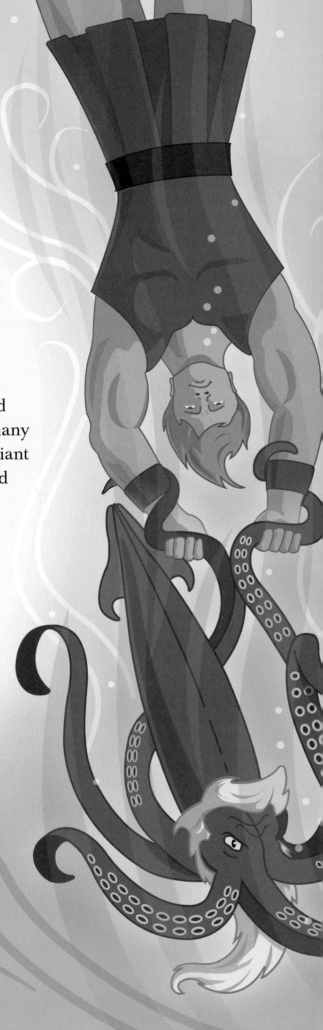

Say Something Technique
Take turns reading a section of text, covering it up, and then saying something about it to your partner. You may say any thought or idea that the text brings to your mind.

"I must find the golden apples," Hercules replied. "It is the last one of many labors I must perform. I must prove myself worthy of being the son of Zeus."

Nereus laughed loudly. He said, "I hope you have to scavenge all over the Earth and never find the garden. It would be a pleasure to see a mighty man like Hercules fail!"

In anger, Hercules grabbed Nereus. He demanded that sea god tell him the location. But Nereus had many tricks. The sea god quickly changed himself into a giant squid. With his many arms, he grabbed Hercules and pulled him down to the deepest depths of the sea.

A giant squid is strong enough to strangle a whale. However, Nereus was no match for Hercules. Even after being dragged a mile underwater in the ocean, Hercules hung on tightly and wrestled the giant sea monster. Eventually, Nereus began losing his strength, and changed himself again, this time into a shark.

What mental images do you have of the different forms that Nereus takes?

246

Floating up to the surface, the shark charged Hercules. Rather than avoid his attacker, Hercules grabbed the shark's body. Both Hercules and Nereus shot up out of the water. Then they landed in the ocean again, splashing so soundly that a tidal wave moved swiftly to shore. As a fierce shark, Nereus tried to bite Hercules in half. Hercules was stronger and held the shark's jaw tightly shut. Nereus swam for hundreds of miles, trying to shake off Hercules. Finally, Nereus became tired and stopped.

"What will you change yourself to be next?" Hercules taunted.

Nereus finally recognized godlike qualities in Hercules. The giant squid and the shark were the strongest creatures of the sea, and Hercules had beaten them both.

"Very well," Nereus said. "The golden apples are in the garden beside the river beyond the two valleys. Ask Atlas to help you, and his daughters will render the dragon harmless." Hercules knew that Atlas was being forced to hold up the Sky and Earth.

How do mental images help you understand this story?

Hercules found Atlas and offered to take his load if Atlas fetched the apples. Atlas had been holding the Earth and Sky for so long that he was thrilled to have Hercules offer some relief. Atlas gave the Sky and Earth to Hercules, and shortly after, he returned with the golden apples.

Atlas said, "I will take these apples to Eurystheus myself. Hold onto the load for a little while longer while I finish your task."

Hercules believed that Atlas would never return. He asked, "Fine, but could you just hold the Sky and Earth for a moment? I need to add some soft padding onto my shoulders."

What mental image do you have of Atlas and Hercules talking?

Atlas agreed. Hercules picked up the apples and ran off before Atlas could stop him.

Hercules presented the golden apples to Eurystheus, and after performing one more task was taken by Zeus to Mount Olympus and declared a god. From that day on, even Hera recognized his good qualities and accepted him as if he were one of her own children.

Think and Respond

Reflect and Write

- You and your partner have read *The Adventures of Hercules on Sea and Land*. Discuss the thoughts and ideas that came to your mind.

- On one side of an index card, describe one of your favorite mental images from the story. On the other side of the index card copy the sentences from the text that brought this image to your mind.

Adjectives in Context

Reread *The Adventures of Hercules on Sea and Land* to find examples of adjectives. Write down the words you find. Then use the adjectives in four sentences that describe Nereus and Hercules locked in battle. Exchange you favorite sentence with a partner.

Turn and Talk

CREATE IMAGES

Discuss with a partner what you have learned so far about creating mental images.

- How do you create mental images?

- How does creating mental images help you better understand what you read?

Choose one of the mental images you created while reading *The Adventures of Hercules on Sea and Land*. Explain to a partner how that image helped you enjoy and understand the story.

Critical Thinking

In a group, brainstorm the characteristics of hero figures. Write your ideas on one side of a piece of paper. Return to *The Adventures of Hercules on Sea and Land*. Write on the other side of the sheet of paper the characteristics of the hero figures in the myth. Then answer these questions.

- Why didn't Nereus want to give Hercules information about the golden apples?

- Why did Nereus change into a giant squid and a shark?

- Why do you think Hercules was able to succeed in completing his tasks?

Glossary

Using the Glossary

Like a dictionary, this glossary lists words in alphabetical order. Guide words at the top of each page show you the first and last word on the page. If a word has more than one syllable, the syllables are separated by a dark dot (•). Use the pronunciation key on the bottom of every other page.

Sample

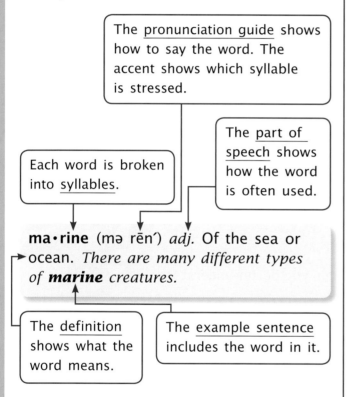

The pronunciation guide shows how to say the word. The accent shows which syllable is stressed.

The part of speech shows how the word is often used.

Each word is broken into syllables.

ma•rine (mə rēn´) *adj.* Of the sea or ocean. *There are many different types of marine creatures.*

The definition shows what the word means.

The example sentence includes the word in it.

Abbreviations: *adj.* adjective, *adv.* adverb, *conj.* conjunction, *interj.* interjection, *n.* noun, *prep.* preposition, *pron.* pronoun, *v.* verb

a•brupt•ly (ə brupt´ le) *adv.* Coming, happening, or ending suddenly. *The man **abruptly** left the room.*

a•maze•ment (ə māz´ mənt) *n.* Great wonder. *I looked at the giant flower with **amazement.***

ar•gu•ment (är´ gyo͞o mənt) *n.* A reason or reasons offered for or against something. *Eliza made a strong **argument** in favor of going to the park.*

banned (bannd) *v.* Having said officially that something cannot be done. *The law **banned** slavery.*

de•ci•bel (de´ sə bəl) *n.* A number representing the relative loudness of a sound. *A sound that is one **decibel** would be difficult to hear.*

de•le•gates (de´ lə gəts) *pl. n.* People sent to speak or act for others. *Our school sent **delegates** to the town meeting.*

De•mo•cra•tic (de´ mə kra´ tik) *adj.* Belonging to the Democratic Party. *My uncle is a member of the **Democratic** Party.*

de•spair (di spâr´) *n.* Loss of hope. *You could see the **despair** on the girl's face.*

domed (dōmd) *v.* Shaped like a dome, or having a rounded roof. *The building's roof was **domed.***

en•er•gy (en´ ər je) *n.* The ability or power to do work. *Running a mile takes a great deal of **energy.***

en·vi·ron·ment (en vī´ rən mənt) *n.* All of the surroundings and conditions that affect the growth of living things. *Many animals adapt to their* **environment.**

ex·ot·ic (eg zä´ tik) *adj.* Strangely beautiful or unusual, often coming from another country. *The zoo had many* **exotic** *birds.*

gen·er·at·ed (jen´ ər āt´ ed) *v.* Produced; caused something to be. *The fire* **generated** *a great deal of heat and smoke.*

gen·er·os·ity (jen´ ər äs´ ə tē) *n.* Willingness to give and share. *Mrs. Collins, our neighbor, is known for her* **generosity.**

gour·met (go͞or mā´) *n.* A person who likes and is a very good judge of fine food. *My father is a* **gourmet.**

in·ter·i·or (in tir´ ē ər) *n.* On the inside. *The* **interior** *of the apartment was very small.*

knead (nēd) *v.* To mix or press dough or clay into a soft mass. *To make many kinds of bread, you have to* **knead** *the dough.*

le·gal (lē´ gəl) *adj.* Created by or based upon law; having to do with the law. *The court ruled that it is every person's* **legal** *right to vote.*

leg·is·la·ture (lej´ əs lā´ chər) *n.* A group of people given the duty and power to make laws. *The state* **legislature** *passed a new tax law.*

lib·er·ty (li´ bər tē) *n.* Freedom. *The American colonists wanted* **liberty.**

ma·rine (mə rēn´) *adj.* Having to do with the sea or ocean. *There are many different types of* **marine** *creatures.*

na·vi·gate (na´ və gāt) *v.* To travel through or over water, air, or land in a ship or aircraft. *A bat is able to* **navigate** *in a dark cave.*

op·po·si·tion (äp´ ə zi´ shən) *n.* A person, group, or thing that is against something. *The storeowners formed a strong* **opposition** *to the new tax.*

pen·sion (pen´ shən) *n.* A regular payment made to a person for service. *My aunt receives a* **pension** *for her service in the military.*

PRONUNCIATION KEY

a	add, map	oi	oil, boy	zh	vision, pleasure
ā	ace, rate	ou	pout, now	ə	the schwa, an
â(r)	care, air	o͝o	took, full		unstressed vowel
ä	palm, father	o͞o	pool, food		representing the
e	end, pet	u	up, done		sound spelled
ē	equal, tree	û	her, sir,		*a* in *above*
i	it, give		burn, word		*e* in *sicken*
ī	ice, write	yo͞o	fuse, few		*i* in *possible*
o	odd, hot	z	zest, wise		*o* in *melon*
ō	open, so				*u* in *circus*
ô	order, jaw				

pe·ti·tion (pə ti´ shən) *n.* A letter or other written document asking that something be changed, often signed by many people. *The townspeople delivered the **petition** to the mayor.*

pho·to·phores (fō´ tə fôrs´) *n.* Body parts in some animals that produce light. *A dragonfish has **photophores** that produce light.*

po·li·tics (pä´ lə tiks) *n.* The work of government. *Mr. Ramos entered **politics** right after college.*

pro·cess (prä´ ses´) *n.* A particular method of doing something. *I have a fast **process** for cleaning my room.*

ra·di·ate (rā´ dē āt) *v.* To send out rays of heat or light. *I could feel the heat **radiate** from the oven.*

re·ac·tion (rē ak´ shən) *n.* An action in response to something. *Mixing the two chemicals caused a surprising **reaction.***

Re·pu·bli·can (ri pu´ bli kən) *n.* Belonging to the Republican Party. *My aunt always votes as a **Republican.***

re·source (rē´ sôrs´) *n.* Something that can be used to meet a need. *Water is an important **resource.***

re·spond (ri spänd´) *v.* To answer or reply. *My mother wanted me to **respond** to her question.*

slug·gish·ly (slug´ ish lē) *adv.* Slowly. *The turtle moved **sluggishly.***

sub·mers·i·ble (səb mur´ sə bəl) *n.* A vessel that can operate under water. *The **submersible** could dive deep into the ocean.*

ten·ta·cle (ten´ tə kəl) *n.* A long, slender, flexible growth near the head or around the mouth of an animal, used for grasping, feeling, or moving. *The octopus used its **tentacle** to grab the starfish.*

W

weal·thy (wel´ thē) *adj.* Having money or riches. *The **wealthy** man lived in a big house.*

Acknowledgements

For permission to reprint copyrighted material, grateful acknowledgment is made to the following sources:

Big Blue by Shelley Gill, illustrations by Ann Barrow. Text © 2003 by Shelly Gill. Illustrations © 2003 by Ann Barrow. Used with permission by Charlesbridge Publishing, Inc. All rights reserved.

from *Chato's Kitchen* by Gary Soto, illustrations by Susan Guevara. Text © 1995 by Gary Soto. Illustrations © 1995 by Susan Guevara. Used by permission of G. P. Putnam's sons, A Division of Penguin Young Readers Group, A Member of Penguin Group (USA) Inc., 345 Hudson Street, New York, NY 10014. All rights reserved.

from *Dangerous Crossing: The Revolutionary Voyage of John Quincy Adams* by Stephen Krensky, illustrated by Greg Harlin. Text © 2005 by Stephen Krensky. Illustrations © 2005 by Greg Harlin. Used by permission of Dutton Children's Books, A Division of Penguin Young Readers Group (USA) Inc., 345 Hudson Street, New York, NY 10014.

Down, Down, Down in the Ocean by Sandra Markle, illustrations by Bob Marshall. Text © 1999 by Sandra Markle. Illustrations © by Bob Marshall. Used with permission by Walker Publishing Co. All rights reserved.

from *Duke Ellington* by Andrea Davis Pinkney, illustrations by Brian Pinkney. Copyright © 1998. Reprinted by permission of Hyperion Books for Children.

from *Give Me Liberty!* By Russell Freedman. Text © 2000 by Russell Freedman. All rights reserved. Reprinted from *Give Me Liberty! The Story of the Declaration of Independence*. Used by permission of Holiday House, Inc.

from *How the U. S. Government Works* by Syl Sobel. Text © 1999 by Sylvan A. Sobel. Illustrations © 1999 by Barrons Educational Series, Inc. Reprinted by arrangement of Barrons Educational Series, Inc., Hauppauge, NY

Papa's Mark by Gwendolyn Battle-Lavert, illustrations by Colin Bootman. Text © 2003 by Gwendolyn Battle-Lavert. Illustrations © 2003 by Colin Bootman. All rights reserved. Reprinted from *Papa's Mark* by permission of Holiday House, Inc.

Unit Opener Acknowledgements

P.2a Washington Crossing the Delaware River, 25th December 1776, 1851 (oil on canvas) (copy of an original painted in 1848) by Leutze, Emanuel Gottlieb (1816–68) © Metropolitan Museum of Art, New York, USA/ The Bridgeman Art Library; p.64a © Gilbert Mayers: Serious Sound, 2005 / SuperStock ; p.126a © Norman Rockwell: How Goes the War on Poverty?, 1965 / Look Magazine / Library of Congress; p.188a © Erich Lessing / Art Resource, NY .

Illustration Acknowledgements

P.8b Carlotta Tormey/Wilkinson Studios; p.13c Thomas Gagliano/Wilkinson Studios; p.14a Judith Hunt/Wilkinson Studios; p.16a Jerry Tiritilli/Wilkinson Studios; p.18a Jerry Tiritilli/Wilkinson Studios; p.20a Jerry Tiritilli/Wilkinson Studios; p.21b Jerry Tiritilli/Wilkinson Studios; p.24a Judith Hunt/Wilkinson Studios; p.28a Ron Mahoney/Wilkinson Studios; p.30a Ron Mahoney/Wilkinson Studios; p.32a Ron Mahoney/Wilkinson Studios; p.42a Joe Boddy/Wilkinson Studios; p.43a Joe Boddy/Wilkinson Studios; p.54a Nancy Zimbalist/Wilkinson Studios; p.58a Tom McNeely/Wilkinson Studios; p.60a Tom McNeely/Wilkinson Studios; p.62a Tomy McNeely/Wilkinson Studios; p.70a Gene Rosner/Wilkinson Studios; p.78b,c Janet Nelson/Wilkinson Studios; p.79b Janet Nelson/Wilkinson Studios; p.80a Janet Nelson/Wilkinson Studios; p.82a Janet Nelson/Wilkinson Studios; p.84b,c,d Thomas Gagliano/Wilkinson Studios; p.88a Stan Gorman/Wilkinson Studios; p.100c Caroline Hu/Wilkinson Studios; p.101c Caroline Hu/Wilkinson Studios; p.104a Robert Eberz/Wilkinson Studios; p.109b George Hamblin/Wilkinson Studios; p.110d George Hamblin/Wilkinson Studios; p.114b Chris Pappas/Wilkinson Studios; p.116a,a Bradley Clark/Wilkinson Studios; p.118a George Hamblin/Wilkinson Studios; p.120a Noah Clay Phipps/Wilkinson Studios; p.122a Noah Clay Phipps/Wilkinson Studios; p.124a Noah Clay Phipps/Wilkinson Studios; p.125b Noah Clay Pgipps/Wilkinson Studios; p.140a,a S.G. Brooks/Wilkinson Studios; p.142a S.G. Brooks/Wilkinson Studios; p.144a S.G. Brooks/Wilkinson Studios; p.145d S.G. Brooks/Wilkinson Studios; p.148a Cynthia Sears/Wilkinson Studios; p.152a Al Lorenz/Wilkinson Studios; p.154a Al Lorenz/Wilkinson Studios; p.156a Al Lorenz/Wilkinson Studios; p.166a Caroline Hu/Wilkinson Studios; p.171c George Hamblin/Wilkinson Studios; p.182a Rob McClurkan/Wilkinson Studios; p.184a Rob McClurkan/Wilkinson Studios; p.186a Rob McClurkan/Wilkinson Studios; p.187b Rob McClurkan/Wilkinson Studios; p.202a S.G. Brooks/Wilkinson Studios; p.204a,b S.G. Brooks/Wilkinson Studios; p.206a S.G. Brooks/Wilkinson Studios; p.207d S.G. Brooks/Wilkinson Studios; p.288a Paula Wendland/Wilkinson Studios; p.229a Paula Wendland/Wilkinson Studios; p.232a Judith Hunt/Wilkinson Studios; p.233d George Hamblin/Wilkinson Studios; p.234a Judith Hunt/Wilkinson Studios; p.235a Judith Hunt/Wilkinson Studios; p.236a Judith Hunt/Wilkinson Studios; p.236d George Hamblin/Wilkinson Studios; p.237b Judith Hunt/Wilkinson Studios; p.238b George Hamblin/Wilkinson Studios; p.240a Rob Doe/Wilkinson Studios; p.244a Brad Schneider/Wilkinson Studios; p.246a Brad Schneider/Wilkinson Studios; p.248a Brad Schneider/Wilkinson Studios; p.249b Brad Schneider/Wilkinson Studios.

Photography Acknowledgements

P.8c ©Kindra Clineff/ Index Stock Imagery; p.8d ©North Wind/North Wind Picture Archives; p.12d Element Photo Shoot; p.12b ©Ian Dagnall/Alamy, TSP 1; p.12b ©Aurora/Getty Images, TSP 1; p.12c ©Chuck Pefley /ipnstock.com, TSP 1; p.13a ©William Owens/Alamy, TSP 2; p.13b ©Tibor Bognar/Alamy, TSP 2; p.23d ©Ace Stock Limited/Alamy; p.26a Element Photo Shoot; p.34a ©Joseph Sohm; Visions of America/Corbis; p.36c ©Bettmann/Corbis; p.37a ©Getty Images; p.37b ©PoodlesRock/Corbis; p.37d ©Joseph Sohm; Visions of America/Corbis 2nd use; p.37c ©Corbis; p.38b Element Photo Shoot; p.38a Courtesy of Historic Urban Plans, Inc.; p.39d ©Annie Griffiths Belt/Corbis; p.41c Element Photo Shoot; p.44a Element Photo Shoot; p.44b ©Bettmann/Corbis; p.45b ©The Granger Collection, New York; p.46a Element Photo Shoot; p.46b ©Bettmann/Corbis; p.47b ©Bettmann/Corbis; p.47d Courtesy of Monticello, Thomas Jefferson Memorial Foundation, Inc.; p.48a Element Photo Shoot; p.48d ©Lester Lefkowitz/Corbis; p.49b ©Bettmann/Corbis; p.50a,d Element Photo Shoot; p.50b ©University of Virginia/Thomas Jefferson Foundation/Edward Owen; p.51d ©Thomas Jefferson Foundation, Inc./Thomas Jefferson Foundation/Edward Owen; p.52a ©By Ian Miles-Flashpoint Pictures/Alamy; p.52d ©Jeff Greenberg/www.agefotostock.com; p.53c ©Andy Crawford/Dorling Kindersley; p.56a Element Photo Shoot; p.56b Photo Courtesy of Valley Forge Visitors Bureau; p.56d ©North Wind/Nancy Carter/North Wind Picture Archives; p.57d ©Colonial Williamsburg Foundation; p.63d ©The Granger Collection, New York; p.66d ©Michael Newman/Photo Edit; p.73d Element Photo Shoot; p.74a,b Element Photo Shoot; p.75a Element Photo Shoot; p.76a Element Photo Shoot; p.76b ©Rick Lew/Jupiter images; p.76c ©Brian Hagiwara/Jupiter Images; p.76d ©Richard Jung/Jupiter Images; p.77d ©Michael Newman/Photo Edit 2nd use; p.82c ©Sprang – StockFood Munich/Stockfood America; p.82d ©Envision/Corbis; p.84a Element Photo Shoot; p.85c ©Lew Robertson/Stockfood America; p.86a ©Dave G. Houser/Post-Houserstock/Corbis;

p.86c ©Corbis; p.86d ©Ahmad Masood/Reuters/Corbis; p.87a ©Bettmann/Corbis; p.87d ©China Newsphoto/Reuters/Corbis; p.90a,c,d Element Photo Shoot; p.90b © Z. Sandmann – StockFood Munich/Stockfood America; p.91a,c Element Photo Shoot; p.91b ©Buntrock–StockFood Munich/Stockfood America; p.91b ©Susie M. Eising FoodPhotography/Stockfood America; p.92a ©Steve Smith/Getty Images; p.92a ©Richard Hutchings/Photo Edit; p.92b ©Z. Sandmann – StockFood Munich/Stockfood America 2nd use; p.93c ©James Worrell/Stockfood America; p.93d ©Jessica Boone/PictureQuest; p.94b Element Photo Shoot; p.94a ©Karin Lau/Shutterstock; p.96a ©Danita Delimont/Alamy;

p.96b ©Dennis MacDonald/Alamy; p.96b ©Joern Sackermann/Alamy; p.100b ©Bettmann/Corbis; p.106b ©Getty Images; p.106b ©Washington Post/reprinted by permission of the DC Public Library/Washington Star newspaper Aug.22, 1948.; p.106d ©Bettmann/Corbis; p.107b ©Bernie Epstein/Alamy; p.108c Element Photo Shoot; p.108b Strauss/Curtis/Corbis; p.109a,d Element Photo Shoot; p.110a,c Element Photo Shoot; p.110b ©Michael Durham/Minden Pictures; p.111b Element Photo Shoot; p.112a,d Element Photo Shoot; p.113d ©Janette Beckman/Corbis; p.113d ©Jose Luis Pelaez, Inc./Corbis; p.117b ©Time & Life Pictures/Getty Images; p.119b ©Boden/Ledingham/Masterfile www.masterfile.com; p.128a ©Michael Ventura/Alamy; p.128b ©Flip Schulke/Corbis; p.128b ©Time & Life Pictures/Getty Images; p.132b Element Photo Shoot; p.132d ©Todd Gipstein/Corbis; p.135d Element Photo Shoot; p.136b,c Element Photo Shoot; p.137b ©The Granger Collection, New York, TSP 26; p.138d ©Bettmann/Corbis; p.139d ©The Granger Collection, New York; p.146a Element Photo Shoot; p.146a,a,a,b,b ©Bettmann/Corbis; p.147b ©Visions of America, LLC/Alamy; p.150b Element Photo Shoot; p.150d ©Associated Press, AP; p.152c ©North Wind Picture Archives/Alamy; p.154c ©Subscription Fund Purchase/Cincinnati Museum of Art; p.155b ©Getty Images; p.155d ©National Portrait Gallery, Smithsonian Institution/Art Resource, NY; p.156d ©Getty Images; p.157b,d Courtesy of the United States Postal Service; p.161a,a,a ©The Granger Collection, NY; p.162a ©Michael Geissinger/The Image Work; p.162c ©Bettmann/Corbis; p.162d ©Associated Press, The White House; p.163c ©Paul Conklin/Photo Edit; p.165d Element Photo Shoot; p.168b,d Element Photo Shoot; p.169d ©James P. Blair/Corbis; p.170a Element Photo Shoot; p.172b Element Photo Shoot 2nd use; p.172d Courtesy of the U.S. Federal Supreme Court; p.173a ©Jose Luis Pelaez, Inc./Corbis; p.174b Element Photo Shoot 3rd use; p.176a,c Element Photo Shoot; p.178c ©Henryk Kaiser/eStock Photo; p.179c ©Stock Connection Distribution/Alamy; p.180d Element Photo Shoot; p.180b ©George Diebold Photography/Getty Images; p.194b ©age fotostock/SuperStock; p.194c ©Jens Nieth/zefa/Corbis; p.195c ©Robert Arnold/Getty Images; p.198a Element Photo Shoot; p.198c ©Jeff Hunter/Getty Images, TSP 37; p.199a ©Georgette Douwma/Getty Images, TSP 38; p.200a Element Photo Shoot; p.200b ©R. Ian Lloyd/Masterfile www.masterfile.com; p.201b ©Onne van der Wal/Corbis; p.208a Element Photo Shoot; p.208d ©Jurgen Freund/naturepl.com; p.209c ©Peter Scoones/Science Photo Library; p.210c ©Norbert Wu/Peter Arnold, Inc.; p.210d ©Helga Lade GmbH, Germany/Peter Arnold, Inc.; p.211b ©David Shale/naturepl.com; p.214d ©Macduff Everton/Corbis; p.215d ©Natalie B. Fobes/National Geographic Society; p.216c,c ©Agence Images/Alamy; p.216c ©Sisse Brimberg/National Geographic Society; p.216c ©OAR/National Undersea Research Program (NURP); p.216d,d ©Agence Images/Alamy 3rd usage; p.216d,d ©OAR/National Undersea Research Program (NURP); p.217c,c ©Agence Images/Alamy 5th usage; p.217c ©James A. Sugar/National Geographic Society; p.217d ©Associated Press; p.218d ©Macduff Everton/Corbis 2nd usage; p.220a ©Peter David / Getty Images; p.224c ©Norbert Wu/Peter Arnold, Inc; p.224d ©Norbert Wu/Minden Pictures; p.230a Element Photo Shoot;

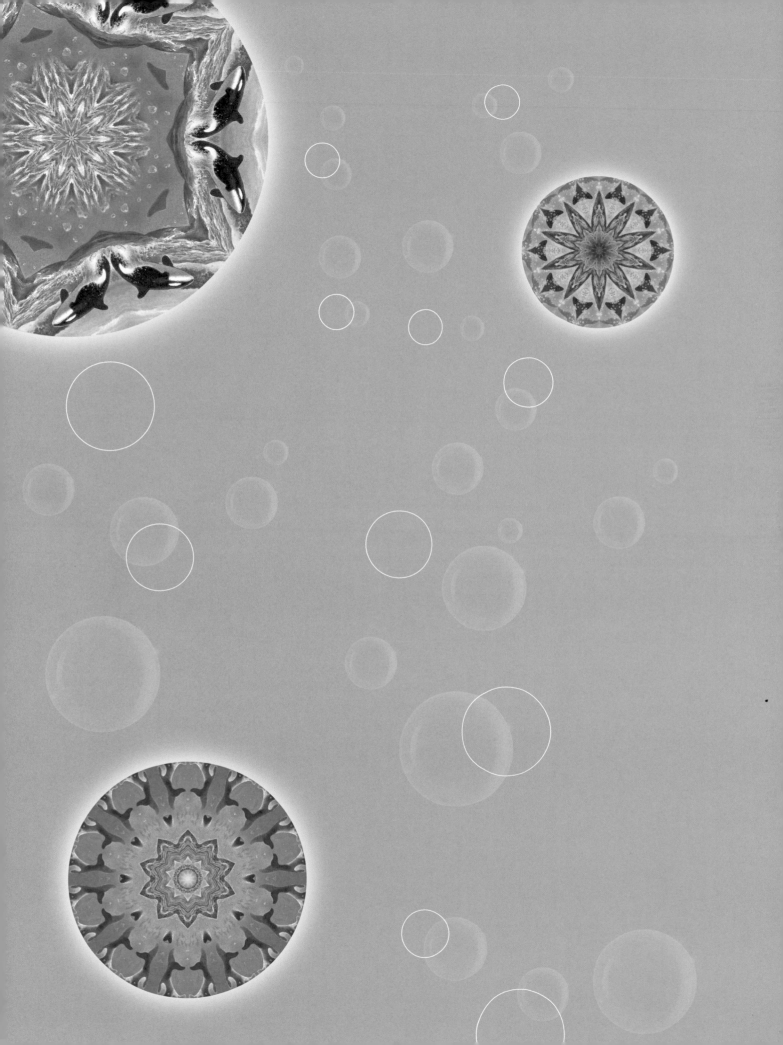